Other Dorset Titles by Countryside Books

EXPLORE DORSET
Harry Ashley

DORSET: A PORTRAIT IN COLOUR
Harry Ashley

THE DORSET VILLAGE BOOK
Harry Ashley

DORSET INNS
Harry Ashley

SMUGGLING IN HAMPSHIRE AND DORSET
Geoffrey Morley

DORSET RAMBLES
Barry Shurlock

THE BOURNEMOUTH COAST PATH
Leigh Hatts

For a complete catalogue of Countryside Books' titles please write to:

The Publicity Manager
Countryside Books
3 Catherine Road
Newbury
Berkshire
RG14 7NA

Dorset Yarns

Harry Ashley

COUNTRYSIDE BOOKS
NEWBURY, BERKSHIRE

First Published 1988

COUNTRYSIDE BOOKS
3 Catherine Road
Newbury, Berkshire

ISBN 1 85306 011 9

Cover illustration by John Baker

Produced through MRM Associates, Reading
Typeset by J&L Composition Ltd, Filey, North Yorkshire
Printed in England by J.W. Arrowsmith, Bristol

For Bumble, a constant companion, loyal and uncomplaining.

Contents

Acknowledgements

THE author wishes to thank friends and acquaintances who have rallied around to search their memories in the preparation of this book of Dorset Yarns. Amongst them The Lord Digby, John Hillier, Hugh Ashley, Erb. E. Elmes, Tas Brackstone, the Library staffs of the *Evening Echo*, Bournemouth and the *Dorset Evening Echo* Weymouth. Finally those who tolerated his demands in the production of the script, including John Baker for the excellent cover picture, Rita Gaywood, Publisher Nicholas Battle, and Editor Margaret Carruthers, and finally Di Pestell who has patiently deciphered and presented another thirty odd thousand words into a readable manuscript.

Introduction

DORSET, with green fields and rich agricultural land, resembles a giant patchwork quilt reaching down from the hills of Shaftesbury and Pilsdon to a fringe of sand and pebble where it meets the surf of the English Channel. This is the background to the yarns featured in this book.

The county has been blessed with splendid storytellers. Sir Frederick Treves, with his whimsical sense of humour, and Arthur Mee have provided volumes on the Dorset folklore in styles that can be easily digested. Treves acknowledged Hutchins' earlier Dorset history, and the Proceedings of the Dorset Natural History and Antiquarian Field Club.

Modern writers have produced valuable additions. David Burnett, in several volumes, features Dorset pictures before and after the coming of the camera, and Rodney Legg, former Editor of the *Dorset County Magazine* and author of countless books, has probably done more to encourage Dorset folk to take an interest in their county than any other author.

My collection of Dorset yarns features many of the better known legends, plus stories gathered myself during a half century of news gathering in the county – first with the *Dorset County Chronicle* and *Southern Times* and, later, with the *Evening Echo*, Bournemouth. Some of the tales were told me as I visited inns for my recent book, *Dorset Inns*.

So join me in the adventures of Charles II's flight through Dorset. Meet the dear old lady of Brownsea, as well as a Swanage Dick Whittington. The characters you will meet range from the Duke of Monmouth to Mr. Melmouth, an early Poole innkeeper and, on the way, you will encounter the naughty nuns of Shaftesbury and many other strange people. Smuggler Gulliver is remembered and even Father Christmas gets a look in.

Each chapter is a complete story so the reader can pick up the book and enjoy a few minutes reading at any time.

Harry W. Ashley
1988

1

Lovey Warne The Smuggler

FEW women have made their mark among the notorious characters who used the high seas to carry out exciting acts of piracy, and the more cunning and profitable trade of smuggling. An exception was Lovey Warne, a shapely young lady from the edge of the New Forest.

Many of the smugglers who kept the aristocracy and wealthy supplied with such necessary products as silks, tobacco, tea and nothing more naughty than brandy, became respected in business. The Court of King George III was on the receiving end of such luxuries when they stayed at Weymouth and it was the King himself who said of the infamous Dorset smuggler, Isaac Gulliver, 'Let Gulliver smuggle as he will', after Gulliver had warned the Royal visitor of a plot on his life.

Into this mainly male world stepped Lovey Warne. Lovey lived with her two brothers on the heights of Crow Hill, north west of Burley. As a young woman she would ride her pony to the mouth of the Avon and the quays at Mudeford and Christchurch where she clambered aboard the vessels under the eye of the Revenue Officers, who probably suspected that her visits aboard were for the satisfaction of sea captains deprived of home comforts through being at sea for long periods. They probably gave her a knowing smile when she stepped ashore, enjoying the waft of her perfume and admiring her colourful bonnets and cloaks. The truth was that she was engaged in a very profitable business, and the flowing cloaks disguised the fact that Lovey left the ships with a much more solid contour than when she arrived. Trips to the moored vessels were pre-arranged, and she would strip off in the captain's cabin and wind the smuggled valuable silks and priceless laces around her body. Then she gallantly left, with the captain perhaps holding her hand to help her ashore. With a wink and a smile at the Revenue men, she hastened to her pony and home to her brothers who, from their cottage warehouse, distributed the goods. So many a fine lady from London to Salisbury sometimes wore silk that had entered the country clinging to Lovey Warne's flesh.

Her seductive smile almost proved her undoing. Stepping ashore wrapped in expensive silk after one such rendezvous with a sea captain, a waiting Revenue man – with thoughts very distant from contraband – found himself compelled to follow Miss Warne. Plucking up courage, he caught up with her and suggested they should visit an inn for a drink.

It would have been stupid for her to have refused and risk angering him, so they entered a Christchurch inn and, to the disgust of customers in the bar, both became merry on gin.

Red-cheeked and excited at his progress, the Revenue man made an investigative caress of Lovey's knee. She brushed him aside but, thinking she was teasing, he made a fresh attempt on her thigh, at the same time putting his other arm around her to constrain her.

Panic-stricken that her amorous partner would soon discover her abnormal girth, she rose up and, whether by accident or design, banged her elbow into his eye and with a stream of oaths fled from the bar. The landlady, who had perceived Lovey's predicament, rushed toward the Revenue man, who was reeling in agony. She and her friends persuaded him that he was seriously hurt and engulfed him in nursing comfort – getting cold compresses to place over his sore eye – and doing all they could to detain him whilst Lovey made her escape.

After this adventure, Lovey's brothers, Peter and John, decided that her dangerous solo quayside assignments must cease and she was given a new task. She became a living warning for the local smugglers. When Peter and John, at their Crow Hill headquarters, had knowledge of smugglers arriving at Avon Beach or Chewton Bunny at Highcliffe when the law men were in the vicinity, Lovey would don a red robe and parade all day on the top of Verely Hill so that the 'Gentlemen of the Night' would move inland by a more eastern route and thus avoid detection.

In nearby Burley, a famous smuggling centre, the ancient Queens Head Inn was the meeting place for the Warne family. To this day you can drink in the flagstoned Warne's Bar and, in this dimly lit room, sit where Lovey Warne spent her evenings. A proud Burley resident will probably regale you with tales of this locally well respected family – especially Lovey Warne – who, to the end of her long life, would still tuck up her skirts and scramble astride a horse with best brandy bottles hanging from a stout belt at the end of an evening's drinking.

2

The Tragedy of the *Halsewell*

CAPTAIN Richard Pierce stood proudly by the wheel of the giant East Indiaman *Halsewell* as she ran down the Thames. The oldest skipper with the Company was making his last voyage and two of his daughters were on board with him. It was the first day of January 1786, a new year and the start of a new voyage to the Coast of Africa and Bombay, transporting soldiers and five other women among the passengers.

The *Halsewell* at 758 tons was a large vessel for those days and as the estuary widened and Pierce piled on more sail, he had no knowledge that within a week his proud ship would be dashing herself to pieces on a Dorset shore.

The vessel nosed into Channel waters and off the Isle of Wight a severe gale caused her to ship a lot of water. The westerly grew in force and by the 4th of January she had several feet of water slopping in her hold, and was rolling so violently that the captain ordered the mizzen mast to be cut down, but his troubles had only just begun – the rolling did not cease and in giving the mainmast similar treatment to the mizzen further reducing sail, five crewmen got entangled in the mass of loose rigging and were dragged overboard and drowned.

Under a jury rig the *Halsewell* made slow progress against headwinds. The next day the Captain saw Portland Bill and in trying to make the shelter of the Island's Roads, found he was too far to the leeward and could only run for Studland, and the shelter of the east facing bay. Nightfall brought further problems because the vessel was now at the mercy of the wind and the captain could not see where he was heading with green seas breaking over his ship. Just before midnight the weather briefly cleared and Captain Pierce saw he was bearing down on St. Aldhelm's Head. He dropped anchor but this only slowed progress and caused the vessel to get into an uncontrollable roll.

Richard Pierce knew then that his *Halsewell* was doomed. The westerly gale was sweeping up from the Atlantic unhindered by any land, driving snow swirled around him and it was bitterly cold. Perhaps he prayed in those last minutes but he was probably too busy and frightened. We shall never know because at 2 a.m. on 6th January *Halsewell* was lifted by a giant wave and thrown onto rocks at Seacombe, west of the Winspit cutting, near St. Aldhelm's Head and Captain Pierce and his daughters perished together with about 170 souls in a night of horror.

Shrieks of terror from every part of the vessel were drowned by the raging storm and the timbers of *Halsewell* split asunder as her bilges stove in on the jagged rocks. Many trapped below decks were swept to their deaths as the vessel split in two and the relentless sea scoured the interior as if searching for bodies.

Seacombe is a lonely place even in summer and on this wild January night, over 200 years ago, no-one saw the incident. In the darkness those who had clambered ashore and were still alive, soon realised that they were beneath a towering jagged cliff and lodged in the mouth of a cave. What happened in the next hour or two is uncertain. Most frightened survivors would, no doubt, have preferred staying with the shattered hull as long as possible, rather than clamber over the slimy rocks and risk being dashed to pieces by the relentless waves. The ship's Chief Officer jumped from the stern and scrambled to the comparative safety of a ledge, but he could find no way of scaling the cliff to raise the alarm.

The shivering and stupefied survivors clung to any shelter they could find on the wallowing wreck until the grey light of dawn threw some light on their predicament. They then realised that if they scrambled ashore to the ledges they would not be seen from the clifftop because of the overhang. Making dashes between the foaming seas, some used spars to form bridges to the cave's ledges and got ashore. But even there the waves continued to harass them and many were literally licked off by the swirling teasing seas as others screamed and clung to each other. The ship's cook and the quartermaster eventually succeeded in scaling the cliff and raised the alarm at a nearby cottage and a band of quarrymen, accustomed to working on the cliffs, were alerted and two were lowered halfway down on ropes to assess the situation and the exact spot of the cave. But even in the long hours of rescue the angry sea did not give up and some survivors with feelingless fingers could not knot the ropes that would have hauled them to safety and they dropped into the icy water or fell to their deaths on the rocks.

At least 70 died, even though they had survived getting ashore – washed away or stiffened by the long night of cold as they waited for the life-saving rope to come their way. It took 24 hours to get the last of the 74 survivors to the clifftop.

When the storm abated, they collected the bodies of those the sea had tossed ashore and laid them to rest in a special cemetery at Seacombe Bottom. Cannons retrieved from the wreckage were set up as a memorial.

Little remains to remind us of that awful night in 1786 but two strange items survived: a mirror, which hangs in the Church at Worth Matravers and a green hour-glass, which can be seen in the County Museum at Dorchester. Sixty years later Charles Dickens was so touched by the *Halsewell* disaster that he used the account of the wreck as the basis for his famous story *The Long Journey*.

The clifftop from Anvil Point to St. Aldhelm's Head is now one of the most beautiful and popular stretches of the Dorset Coast Walk. So those who come to enjoy the sea breezes along the undulating clifftop can pause for a while at Seacombe Bottom and recall that winter night of terror when the *Halsewell* met her end.

3

Bincombe's Hour of Glory

YOU will not find Bincombe listed in any organised tour of Dorset. This tiny village, nestling in a valley formed by the great Ridgeway near Weymouth, is on a narrow road to nowhere, a road which leads off the Ridgeway hill at its notorious hairpin bend to a group of thatched cottages beside a 13th century church.

Off the beaten track, it slumbers almost unaware of the world beyond the hill and has always seemed reluctant to comply with even the basic needs of modern living, with no village shop or even street lighting.

The shire horses which once trudged home at sundown in single file through the narrow street have long gone. Sometimes it is so quiet that you could be forgiven for thinking the village had been evacuated, and the bird song to the accompaniment of the west wind, whistling through the trees higher up the hillside, is the only sound.

But little Bincombe once had an hour of glory. Before the Second World War, in the days when wireless was the main means of communication, it was a ritual on Christmas Day for the family to gather around the wireless. These were early days of that media and it seemed like a miracle as throughout the morning there were link-ups with places all over the world.

From Birmingham to Bethlehem everyone heard what was happening on the Holy Day. Lonely lighthouse keepers and London's Trafalgar Square crowds were part of the world-wide, three-hour radio tour which culminated with the King's

Christmas message broadcast to subjects in all parts of Britain's then Empire.

In the year 1930 the Dorset farmer, author and wireless personality, Ralph Wightman – whose talks in broad Dorset dialect were well-known on the air – contributed to the programme by describing Christmas from a Dorset village. He chose Bincombe.

Ralph Wightman farmed in the Piddle Valley and was the voice of Dorset. He regularly broadcast talks on the countryside in the rich dulcet Dorset dialect. He was one of the leading media personalities of the 1930s. During his broadcast the whole world heard the peal of Bincombe's bells calling the people to worship. Ralph stood at the gate of the church and welcomed the arriving villagers. He described and named them. Farmers, farmhands and shepherds with their families obeyed the call of the bells, as the shepherds of Bethlehem once obeyed the star and, over the airways, the world heard the singing of the first hymn, to the accompaniment of a throaty organ.

For a few brief minutes on that Christmas Day the whole world was aware of Bincombe in Dorset, a little hamlet in the shadow of a hill, within earshot of the English Channel waves which, during storms, can be heard grinding into the Chesil Bank of pebbles at nearby Portland.

For a few brief minutes Bincombe was united with the little town of Bethlehem, and the countryfolk enjoyed their hour of fame. Then the village went back to its sleepy obscurity. And today few villagers even remember that it ever happened.

4

The Abbotsbury Evidence

NOW that the extra marital affairs and sex escapades of humble citizens and Royals alike are regularly recorded in our newspapers, the 18th century national scandal of the teenage girl and the brothel keeper would probably not even make the inside pages. But, in the 1750s, the Elizabeth Canning case had famous novelist, Henry Fielding, the author of *Tom Jones* and a forthright paragon of morals, and the Lord Mayor of London publicly at loggerheads in a seamy litigious wrangle. The locations of this intrigue prominently featured west Dorset villages, in the poor wretched defendant's alibi.

When an attractive girl accuses an aged ugly gypsy woman of forcing her into prostitution, it is human nature that the girl would win most sympathy, whatever the facts proved. A case of 'Give a dog a bad name and hang him', but the situation was not as straightforward as this introduction implies.

Eighteen year old Elizabeth Canning, in service in the city of London, was given permission to visit her uncle in Moorfields on New Year's Day 1752. She never reached her destination and turned up four weeks later exhausted and dishevelled, saying she had been kidnapped and taken to a house at Enfield and made a prisoner for immoral purposes. The 'Madam' of the bawdy house, Susannah Wells, was not running a sophisticated establishment. In fact most of the women were gypsies and one, Mary Squires, was a hideous figure that would not easily be forgotten – particularly by the witnesses she would eventually call on to establish her alibi. She was large, tall and very ugly. Her weather-beaten face was dominated by an unusually large lower lip. Over her rough serge clothes she wore a waistlength cape, and she was nearing her three score and ten years of life.

Mother Wells and Mary Squires were arrested on the sworn complaint of Canning and charged with assault and putting the plaintiff in bodily fear, but the course of justice followed a strange pattern. Sub judice seemed to be unheard of and the lead-up to the trial was carried out like a General Election campaign, with the supporters of the brothel keepers on one side and the 'sweet' young Canning on the other, issuing pamphlets stating their case.

The situation was well to the liking of the 'do-gooder' Fielding, a magistrate as well as an author, but poor Squires and Wells were championed by 'Sir' John Hill, a quack doctor and bit of a buffoon, whose utterings appealed to the public ... but he had no great standing. His knighthood was, in fact, a Swedish Order. Arguments for and against the accused were aired not only in the press, but in the taverns of the town.

The two women were found guilty at the eventual trial. Mother Wells received the terrible torture of branding and Mary Squires was sentenced to be hanged. It seemed rough justice and the poor gypsy could not have been treated worse had she committed murder. However, the sentence was held up because a more creditable champion came to her rescue. Her knight in shining armour was none other than the Lord Mayor of London, Sir Crisp Gascoyne, Master of the Brewers Company.

Squires not only claimed that over the period she was accused of abducting Canning in London she was, in fact, visiting inns in west Dorset with her daughter Lucy and son George, but produced witnesses to prove that she had been at Winyards Gap, South Perrett and Abbotsbury, amongst other villages, throughout the period of the abduction. They were making their way to Abbotsbury so that Lucy could be re-united with her sweetheart, William Clarke a young shoemaker.

An honest lad, he eventually came to the trial of Squires and told of the enjoyable New Year celebrations. He brought with him a host of friends including the blacksmith, Melchisedeck Arnold, and Hugh Bond, the schoolmaster. There were innkeepers from Litton Cheney and South Perrett, and people from all walks of life swearing on oath that the Squires family were in Dorset over the New Year period. Alice Farnham, daughter of the landlord of the Three Horseshoes at Winyards Gap, remembered serving them bread and cheese and beer on 30th December, and particularly noted the difference between the gypsy, Mary Squires, and her daughter – 'a clean girl wearing a white gown and red cloak'.

They all had a rough time in the witness box and were treated as liars. The term 'Abbotsbury evidence' became well known in London to signify a person was telling lies. In fact, one prosecution witness in court testified 'All people of Abbotsbury, including the vicar, are thieves, smugglers and plunderers of shipwrecks'.

That was quite near the truth, for it was common practice for coastal folk to be mixed up in 'The Free Trade', and it is most likely that local smugglers, probably Isaac Gulliver himself, were paying the high cost of witnesses' expenses.

William Clarke paid dearly for his love and loyalty to his sweetheart and when Squires was sentenced, he was arrested on a perjury charge. Londoners, shocked by the scandal and firmly siding with Canning, publicly abused the Dorset witnesses in the streets. At this point, a few broad-minded citizens began to have doubts. Supposing Elizabeth Canning had really sneaked off for a naughty weekend which turned into a month long orgy? What better alibi than to say she had been abducted by known prostitutes. Sir Crisp Gascoyne – remember he was in the brewing trade – could not believe that so many publicans and simple living people in the Dorset villages would perjure themselves to save a dishevelled gypsy. He started his own investigation and contacted the vicar of Abbotsbury, James Harris. From the information received, he was sure that justice was not being done.

The outcome was the postponement of the execution of Mary Squires and at the perjury trials of young Clarke, John Gibbons, an Abbotsbury innkeeper, and Thomas Grenville, landlord of the Lamb and Flag at Coombe Bissett where the Squires family spent the night of 14th January, all were acquitted.

Although the Squires family proved beyond doubt that they were enjoying their Dorset pub crawl at the very time that Canning swore Mary Squires kept her without outer clothes at the bawdy house, the London mob did not want to be done out of their hanging party and rioted in the streets when Sir Crisp started his investigation. The full truth will never be known, but the King was petitioned and Elizabeth Canning was eventually brought to trial, convicted of perjury and sent to a penal settlement in the American Colonies for seven years. Surviving it, she married a rich American in Connecticut – proving again that crime does sometimes pay!

Gypsy Mary Squires received a free pardon, but there was little they could do for Susannah Wells who had to wear the scar of her branding for the rest of her life.

So if you visit the lonely hilltop corner of Dorset where the road crests at Winyards Gap and soon twists downhill into the lush Somerset countryside, sit a while on the terrace of the Winyards Gap Inn, which has long replaced the Three Horseshoes of this story, and think back over 230 years and visualise a strange trio struggling up the hillside on the eve of a New Year. An intensely ugly old gypsy woman in old clothes, her bright eyed daughter, nicely groomed, and her son in a red waistcoat and a long greatcoat, innocently strolling into one of the great scandals of the 18th century.

5

King Charles in Flight

ROYALTY have made a habit of indulging in unusual and amusing behaviour in Dorset. King George III popularised sea bathings at Weymouth, and the plight of Charles Stuart, King of England, as he fled from the Battle of Worcester in 1651 to find a boat for France, led him into Dorset escapades which would provide scenarios for the scriptwriters of Aldwych farces and 'Carry On' films. Even Charles himself, in the latter part of his life, regaled his dinner guests with his Dorset adventures.

In his flight he had to give up any idea of getting a boat out of Bristol. So, accompanied by Lord Wilmot – an old friend – he journeyed south to reach the Dorset coast. They planned to stay at the home of Colonel Wyndham, who was friendly to the King's cause, at Trent in north west Dorset, in a house which had a secret room that could be used as a hiding place for emergencies. He concealed himself in this room while Col. Wyndham went in search of a boat at Lyme Regis, 30 miles away. Eventually a sea captain named Stephen Limbry, who was about to sail for St. Malo, was contacted and – avoiding the dangerous topic of Royalists in this pro-Roundhead part of the country – Wyndham struck a deal for the conveyance of two 'merchants' to France.

Now the plot thickens because a different lie was told at Charmouth by Wyndham's servant who had been sent to book rooms at the Queens Armes Inn. The landlady was thrilled by the romantic story that the servant's young master was eloping with a young lady of gentle birth whose family opposed the union, and was delighted to keep the secret and be part of the intrigue.

Back at Trent events were not going too well. Charles, unable to forget his rank, complained bitterly when the church bells rang out and disturbed his peace. He did not know that they were tolling and the villagers rejoicing because a Parliamentary trooper had arrived boasting that he had personally killed Charles Stuart! News had also leaked out in the village that a stranger was staying at the big house, so on the Sunday Lord Wilmot had to be paraded in church, much against his will, because such an activity was far from his usual way of life.

Next day the escaping party left for Charmouth. Charles was disguised as a mounted servant with a Miss Juliana Coningsby riding behind him as his mistress, closely followed by Lord Wyndham and Wilmot. In the bar of the Queens Armes at Charmouth, Juliana and Henry, Lord Wilmot, played the sweethearts' role, holding hands lovingly in the bar. The landlady, Mistress Wade, peeped around the door – her heart warming at the thought of the romantic elopement. The events which followed were pure farce. Limbry's boat did not turn up, as promised, because in the best comedy tradition, he had lost his trousers! Mrs. Limbry, suspicious that one of the passengers her husband was about to take to France was indeed Charles Stuart, and having heard while shopping that it was death to anyone who shielded him, feared for her husband's safety. She not only hid his trousers, but locked him in a bedroom. It is said that he raved and hammered on the door but his wife threatened to disgrace him by running into the street screaming if he did not shut up.

Came the dawn and almost in panic, and assured that the boat would not come, the King and Juliana set out to return to Trent, via Bridport, but a diligent ostler noticed that shoes on some of the horses had been affixed in Worcester. He rushed to report his news to the local parson. The pompous divine, who happened to be the great grandfather of John Wesley, hastened to the inn and this strange conversation took place with the landlady who, by this time, was confused and saddened by the turn of events. 'Margaret,' he said with authority, 'I hear that you are a maid of honour'. Perplexed, she replied: 'What do you mean by that Mr. Parson?' 'Charles Stuart lay last night at your house', continued the cleric in a severe and accusing manner, 'and kissed you when he departed, so that now you cannot but be a maid of honour.' He waited expecting her to throw herself to the ground in remorse but Margaret, who had obviously enjoyed every minute of the interlude, drew herself up and with emotion replied, 'If I believed it was the King, as you say it was, I would think the better of my lips all the days of my life.'

A hue and cry had started but the chasing Roundheads racing off to Bridport believed that Juliana Coningsby was Charles in disguise. The royal party eluded the pursuers by taking a northbound lane out of the town, and eventually reached the safety of Trent after nearly being caught at Broadwindsor. The belief that Charles was dressed as a woman caused another amusing interlude for the aged Sir Hugh Wyndham, who lived at nearby Pilsdon and was an uncle of Col. Wyndham. The troops stormed his house in error and held the fuming Sir Hugh, who had no knowledge that Charles was in Dorset. The ladies of the house were forced to undress because the Roundheads believed Charles was amongst them disguised.

After the excitement of the few days in Dorset the next we hear is that Charles and Wilmot had arrived at distant Shoreham in Sussex. On 15th October the £60 fee, offered for the passage to France, eventually changed hands and Charles boarded a coal-carrying vessel which made a regular run from Shoreham to Poole. Tattersal, the owner and Captain of the brig *Surprise*, deviated from his run and carried a thankful Charles to Fecamp in France with little fuss.

Charles did not forget the sea captain who had so loyally served him or the blackened brig *Surprise* because, after the

Restoration in 1660, the little vessel was sailed to the Thames, then 'dollied up' and anchored off Whitehall. She was renamed *Royal Escape* and registered as a 'fifth rate' – literally a Royal yacht. Tattersal was retained as her Master with a pension of £100 a year, a job for life, and the proud little ship was still afloat until 1791, retaining her honour for 140 years.

6

The Artistic Murderess

THE Romanesque St. Peter's Church in The Grove at Portland is unique and awesome. This stone-built edifice at the heart of a complex, formerly the island's convict prison, was built and furbished by Victorian convicts. The same men who daily descended the hill taking massive blocks of oolite to the shore as they went about the dangerous and backbreaking task of building a vast breakwater to form the island's naval harbour.

A text on the church wall reads 'Render unto them a Recompense O Lord'. Try to visualise embezzlers, thieves and brutal thugs in arrow-stamped clothing, not only fashioning the walls and roof of this prison church with precision and care in the 1870s, but also, out of the solid blocks of stone, creating and carving one of the finest pulpits in the county with a matching lectern. A little later, convict C. W. Brown, an artist in wood, added the Litany Desk. The church was consecrated in 1872. The Service colours, dusty and paper-thin, which hang from the walls of the semi-circular chancel, add to the awesome atmosphere. The tattered remains of a flag laid up by the Australian Imperial Force in 1918 when they left the nearby Verne Citadel, is flanked by a White Ensign and a Union Jack, both used in the First World War. They are blackened and torn and would probably fall to pieces if touched.

We are not told the names of all the convicts who took part in this unique project, but we do know that the mosaic pavement in the Sanctuary, styled after a pavement in Rome, an intricate repeated pattern in black and white, was created by a young woman who carried out one of the most brutal and horrendous murders of the 19th century. She was the notorious Constance Kent.

On 30th June 1860 the body of Francis Saville Kent, not quite 4 years old, was found terribly mutilated in a cesspit in the garden of the Kent family home at Rode in Somerset. Although it was obvious that someone in the household had committed the murder, authorities made no arrest, yet the whole family were under suspicion.

As the investigation progressed, the father sought another home and the murdered child's nursemaid turned grey in a period of weeks but the boy's older sister, 16 year old Constance, seemed unmoved by the tragedy and showed no fear or emotion when questioned. A London detective had suspicions that she had committed the crime but no-one believed his theory and, in spite of a public outcry and questions asked in the House of Commons, the case was shelved unsolved. Local and London police were baffled and there were even letters in *The Times*.

The family broke up and Constance was sent abroad to a boarding school, returning to this country five years later to enter a convent at her own request. As she was about to take Communion shortly before being finally received into the Order, she requested an audience with the Mother Superior and asked if she might make a confession. Paper and pen were produced and she poured out her terrible secret.

She said she had been hurt by scornful remarks made by her stepmother regarding the first Mrs. Kent (Constance Kent's mother). She had meditated revenge and, knowing how fond the second wife was of her baby son, Francis, decided that the greatest hurt she could render her stepmother was to destroy him. The statement then described the most brutal of murders, carried out with unbelievable cunning. She had stolen one of her father's razors and hidden it in her bedroom. Candles and matches were concealed in an outhouse ready for the fatal night in which she had retired to bed as usual but had gone downstairs after midnight and opened a window. Silently creeping upstairs, she had taken the child from his cot where he slept next to his nurse and quietly carried him downstairs to the open window. Lifting him through, she had conveyed him to the shed and, with the razor, committed the horrible murder. Constance then had calmly covered up her crime, returning the razor to its cupboard and destroying her blood-stained nightdress. In spite of her apparent cool, she nursed this terrible secret for over five years.

The police were called to the convent and Constance Kent was brought to Salisbury for trial and was sentenced to death. It is said that the whole Court was distressed and the Judge broke down when he put on the black cap.

Within a fortnight the sentence was commuted to penal servitude for life and Constance Kent was sent to Portland Prison. The fact that she had wanted to enter a convent and later spent her prison life designing and laying beautiful mosaics for many churches, including the Bishop's Chapel at Chichester and The Sanctuary at East Grinstead, leads us to believe that she was suffering remorse for her wicked crime. Up in the gaunt prison on the top of the Island she had plenty of time to muse in the lonely bleak stone fortress which feels the force of Channel gales from east and west.

She served 20 years in the prison and at the age of 41 was released. On the day of her release from prison, clutching the paper parcel containing her personal possessions, she sat in the little train puffing along in the shadow of the awesome Chesil Beach, bringing her to the mainland at Weymouth: a lonely aging woman who had little knowledge of life in the working world. From a village upbringing she had only known schooling and the convent, and was still a very young woman when she was sent to prison. From that time all trace of her was lost. In similar circumstances today the popular press would be queueing up to buy her life story, but these were the days long before cheque book journalism.

It is possible that she may have made a brief appearance in Rode, where her tragic tale began, because one day a stranger – a woman dressed all in black – walked into the village. After calling at the old inn, she was observed standing silently outside the former Kent family home. She spoke to no-one and, after a few minutes, she turned, walked slowly out of the village and vanished into oblivion.

7

The Muddlecombe Crazy Gang

LANDLORD Gordon Sansom gazed from the window of the New Inn on Wareham Quay. They were clearing out the old granary and there amongst the rubbish was Wareham's ancient wooden fire engine. 'Just the thing for a carnival', he mused, and contacted a few friends. They included Ted Brennan, a van driver and grandson of a clown, 'Erb E. Elmes, a maintenance engineer and conjuror who had won the Wessex Magical Association's Comedy Shield three years running, corporation worker Sid Lumber whose sad face made him a natural comedian, and George Cox who owned a horse and cart. That was over 50 years ago – June 1933 – and the men met in the bar of the inn and formed the Muddlecombe Crazy Gang. Unlike traditional carnival tableaux, they decided they would do their act on and off the wagon, involving the crowds in their antics.

That summer they began to set the pattern for a carnival comedy act that was to become famous. The Council fire engine started a caper which made millions laugh – a jest that has gone around the world. No Wessex carnival was complete without the Muddlecombe Gang and the prizes began to accumulate as their fame spread. The Fire Brigade was followed by the Muddlecombe Policemen, Laundry, Brewery, Bus Company, Boy Scouts and the Grannydears Band.

The acting off the wagon caused an amusing situation at Poole. There had been a long wait for the judges. A very elegant group were on a wagon portraying 'The Women of all

Nations'. Britannia in a long white robe was atop the tableau and obviously in some discomfort. The Muddlecombe Gang were 'firemen' and scattering the crowd with small amounts of water from their buckets. A request was made for one of the buckets to ease Britannia's predicament, and at the moment the bucket was being handed back to the Gang, Gordon Sansom came up showing anger because the Gang were not acting and the judges were in sight. Snatching the bucket, he threw the contents over the heads of the crowd!

There was a near tragedy at Wareham River carnival shortly after the war, and the crowds thought it was all part of the act. The Gang, dressed as pirates, emerged from the New Inn in a drunken state and, boarding the larger of two punts, pushed out into the river. One of the members dressed in 'drag' came to the quay pushing a pram. Seeing the sad-faced Sid Lumber, 'she' claimed that he was the father of her 'child'. The man in drag took the second punt and, as he boarded the larger punt, his portly form was too much for the already overloaded boat and it slowly sank – to the joy of the crowd. As the Gang slowly went down in seven feet of water, veteran Sid gripped the arm of a companion. 'I can't swim Harry', he announced. The crowd roared encouragement as the pirates managed to tow Sid into the shallows – then breathless and shaking, a wry smile crossed his lips. As red and black make-up ran down his cheeks, he quipped: 'That's the first time I've been in the bloody "oggin" since Gallipole'!

All the original members of the Gang are now dead except 'Erb Elmes who lives by the riverside at Wareham, lovingly thumbing through thick albums full of the Gang's escapades over 50 years, some making headlines. Such as the night the Grannydears Band gave a rendering of *The Happy Wanderer* in the sedate lounge of the Crown Inn at Blandford; and the Swanage sensation when old 'Coxer' lit a fire in an oil drum on his cart with petrol and gunpowder. There was a mild explosion and a black faced 'Coxer' was screaming 'I've lost my bloody moustache'. It was not only his moustache that was missing, but his eyebrows and half the skin on his face as well.

'Erb's son and a few friends keep up the tradition today, and at the Wareham carnival in 1984 they found a horse and cart and celebrated 50 years of Muddlecombe with the same laundry sketch the Gang performed in 1934, and old 'Erb was hoisted on to the wagon to wield the same flat iron he had used half a century before.

8

Hardy's Lost Lass

THOMAS Hardy wove many stories of intense love in his poetry and prose. His own life certainly did not lack romance. In his early twenties, life in London as an architect made him ill, so he returned to his native Wessex and to his family's cottage in Upper Bockhampton, near Dorchester, for a life of serenity and quietness. At 27 he had his first passionate love affair, with a sixteen year old girl, the daughter of a family closely connected to his own.

Tryphena Sparkes was beautiful with her black hair and dark eyes. She lived in Puddletown, not a great distance to walk from Hardy's own cottage – especially when love is in the air. Even those with the simplest of imaginations can envisage Thomas peering longingly from the tiny windows beneath the thatched eaves, his eyes eagerly following the wending woodland path which leads from the back of the cottage towards Puddletown, where he could meet Tryphena and woo her. At first, the path is quite bright but the open light quickly gives way to the penumbra of the woods. Today the brambles may have been cut back to make way for others to grow, the tree-roots which surface along the journey may now be a little shinier having been polished by countless wandering feet, the overhanging branches may reach even further across the track. But still they shed not only their shadows but their leaves – to lie dead, slowly rotting as they are reclaimed by the soil. Basically, though, nature and atmosphere remain untouched and unmodified. Who knows, it could even be that the same bluebells still carpet the undergrowth in spring – splashes of blue against the darkened ground.

It's an attractive walk, and easy for today's casual wanderer to imagine the lightness of Hardy's heart as he regularly strode to meet his love. Easy to imagine too, the love-filled couple, lingering affectionately through the woodland glades, hands, like the brambles, tightly entwined, lips gently caressing. Always ahead is the backcloth of bright green with the closer trees harshly and forcefully silhouetted darkly against it. High and low, the birds whistle up their sounds to the world of music, budding rhododendrons and green shoots of fern promise the certainty of beauty to come, the fresh smell of dank moss wafts through the tunnel – with only the light of love at the end. To the couple, lost in each other's eyes, these natural things go unnoticed, and not even the gentle breeze, which rustles the leaves, can cool the inner warmth of affection.

Like most passionate affairs, Hardy's didn't stand the test of time. Tryphena, after five years, returned his engagement ring and it has never been known for certain whether or not she bore his child. Such suggestions, consistent with Victorian propriety, were vehemently denied, though it may be that the couple even went through some kind of private wedding service, with only God as witness. The effect of her loss on Hardy was intense – in later life, he wrote about her as his 'lost prize', and she is certainly the model for Sue Bridehead in his final and much-maligned novel *Jude The Obscure*. In fact, most of the heroines in his novels, such as Tess of the d'Urbevilles and Eustacia Vye in *The Return Of The Native*, reflect some aspect of his beloved Tryphena, who slipped from his devoted and caring grasp to marry another. The author's entire remaining life was influenced by her, and his undying disappointment in the eventual failure of their relationship is evident in much of his later writing. The effect of the friendship is a fine example of how fiction is conceived in the womb of truth.

If you walk that path – share a little of Hardy's joy and his sadness – emotions often closely aligned. Human love, as he found, can be fleeting and frail – but nature, as the path illustrates, lives on, enduring and forthright.

9

Tolpuddle & The Martyrs

THE memory of the Tolpuddle Martyrs – those six Dorset farm labourers who dared to challenge their masters and demand a living wage in 1833 – has been neglected by the county. Whatever political thoughts Dorset folk may have, the interlude is remembered throughout the world as one of the roots of Trade Unionism, and foreign visitors flock to the village just to stand on the green where the six men met and decided their historical course of action. Meetings which led to their imprisonment and transportation to a penal colony. And yet many local youngsters have never heard the story.

The six men of Dorset were George Loveless, 41 years of age, his brother James, 29, Thomas Standfield, 51, his son John Standfield, 25, James Brine, 25 and James Hammett. The latter was always the odd man out. He was the only one of the six not connected with Methodism and, when they were eventually brought home by public demand, he was the only one to settle back in the village.

They were sentenced to transportation because they had administered an oath, illegal under the Mutiny Act of 1797, but that, of course, was the excuse.

The labourers' lot was not a happy one in the 1830s. In succeeding years wages were reduced from nine shillings a week in 1830 to seven shillings in 1833. Threatened that a further reduction to six shillings was about to take place, the Dorset men decided it was time to act. The six were exceptionally literate. All could read and write and their leader, George

Loveless, was a man of outstanding character. Beneath the shade of a sycamore tree on the village green, the labourers met to decide how to come to terms with their employers. They used the vicar of Tolpuddle as an intermediary, and promises were made to the workers and not kept.

The Tolpuddle men turned for advice to the Grand National Consolidated Trade Union, and two officials of that body came to Tolpuddle. As a result, the Friendly Society of Agricultural Labourers was formed.

It was the bizarre initiation ceremony which members had to undergo that proved to be their downfall. It seems out of character that these religious and intelligent men held such a ceremony in the upper room of Thomas Standfield's cottage, and stranger still that Methodist local preacher, George Loveless, allowed it. Farm labourers were blindfolded and told to swear an oath on the Bible that they would advance the aims of the Society and not reveal the names of other members. As the blindfold was removed, they were confronted with pictures representing a skeleton and death the reaper – thought to be a reminder of man's end. The ceremony concluded with the reading of a passage from the Bible, prayers and the singing of a hymn.

Whether intentional or not, there was a spy in the group. John Lock, a gardener in the employ of one of the landowners, Squire Frampton of Moreton, told his employer of the ceremony – probably fearing the loss of his job.

Landowners and magistrates became alarmed and, fearing riots, Frampton sought guidance from Lord Melbourne, the Home Secretary. He referred him to an Act of Parliament which was directed against seditious meetings, and one of the penalties under the Act was for the taking of an illegal oath. He suggested: 'Perhaps you will be able to make an example by such means'.

On 20th February 1834 a caution was printed on the front page of the *Dorset County Chronicle* which threatened transportation for seven years for anyone organising 'illegal societies of unions to which they bind themselves by unlawful oaths.'

George Loveless and his five friends were arrested and thrown into gaol. As the news leaked out, support for the six came from many quarters, including Lord Portman of Bryanstone who told Squire Frampton that he thought they were over-reacting.

The magistrates found a case to answer and the six were taken to the cells below the court room to await trial.

Justice Baron Williams was making his first appearance as an Assize Judge and the jury was heavily weighted against the six – all being farmers – and the Judge showed no favours. The Tolpuddle men were betrayed, even if reluctantly, by two of their friends who had been initiated, although it is possible that one, Edward Legg, was planted by the landowners.

Then an incident occurred which historians seem to ignore. The Judge would not let Loveless speak on the prisoners' behalf, so he passed to the Judge a scrap of paper which was quickly read and tossed aside. Had Loveless been allowed to proclaim that speech in Court, it might have changed the course of justice. Loveless was a powerful orator. He preached the gospel on the Methodist circuit each Sunday, plodding to little country chapels, such lonely places as Crossways and Dick O'the Banks. These were his words: 'My Lord, if we have violated any law, it was not done intentionally. We have injured no man's reputation, character, person or property; we are uniting together to preserve ourselves, our wives and our children from utter degradation and starvation. We challenge any man or number of men to prove that we have acted or intended to act different from the above statement.'

Had Loveless uttered those words in the small courtroom at Dorchester, now preserved as a memorial to the six, every newspaper – including the Tory press who seemed to be supporting them – would have found more copy in that speech than all the disgruntled Judge's comments. When he sentenced them, he admitted they were being made an example of.

By the time national reaction could be known, the Tolpuddle

six were on the high seas suffering the appalling conditions of the convict ships.

A meeting was held in the Metropolis and the London Central Dorchester Committee was formed and drew up a motion protesting at the conduct of the trial and the severity of the sentence. They organised a demonstration at Copenhagen Fields, which was then an open space on which Kings Cross Station now stands. About 40,000 sympathisers took part and they produced a petition containing over half-a-million names. Meanwhile the six were facing their new life on the other side of the world. Loveless, who because of illness had sailed on a later ship, *The William Metcalf*, was sent to Hobart in Tasmania and worked on a chain gang. Later the State's Governor showed some consideration and had him transferred to the Governor's farm. He even asked Loveless to send for his family and settle there. The other five arrived earlier on the convict ship, *Surrey*, and were split up to labour on farms in New South Wales. James Hammett was sold for £1 and was forced to walk hundreds of miles to his workplace.

The Tolpuddle case was raised in Parliament and eventually, after a long struggle, full pardon was granted to all six in 1836. It was another three years before they were all home in this country. All except Hammett attended a celebratory dinner in London and, from a special fund set up for them, they were given farms in other parts of the country. They found it difficult to settle and later emigrated to Canada – all except the odd man out, James Hammett, who lived out his life in Tolpuddle.

The sad outcome of this trade union saga is the fact that the martyrs' trial and tribulations did little good, and a decade after the event the weekly wages for farm labourers in Dorset were still only 7s /6d.

Tolpuddle is one of Dorset's loveliest villages. Deeply thatched cottages surround the little village green near the banks of the gentle river Piddle, flowing beside the square towered church.

It would be satisfying to record that the village had been bypassed and left as a peaceful shrine to the martyrs. Instead the authorities widened and straightened the fast east/west main road, which runs through its heart, and destroyed the ancient inn because it was in the way. But once a year Tolpuddle is remembered. On a Sunday in July, leading trade unionists and politicians march through the village headed by a brass band and followed by the massive colourful Victorian banners of trade union groups, supported by members from numerous trades. They then crowd together to hear the speeches, which are often not as sincere as the words spoken there over 150 years ago.

10

The Fossil Woman of Lyme

SCHOOL children, many of them enjoying their first taste of life away from home, come to Lyme Regis to study geology and search for fossils.

The unstable cliffs of black mud east and west of Lyme Regis are famous for the fossils which have been revealed after a succession of landslides in the 19th and 20th centuries. Although beguiled with stories of how a young girl, Mary Anning, became famous for digging up an Ichthyosaurus (fish lizard), millions of years old, most of them are content to get as filthy as possible and know they will not be chastised for it.

Lyme revels in the story of the Fossil Woman, a sad story of a lonely spinster. Mary Anning inherited her love of fossil hunting from her father who supplemented his earnings as a carpenter by collecting fossils in the cliffs and selling them. He took his two children, Joseph and Mary, with him on his Sunday morning excursions.

The 18th century was drawing to a close, sea bathing was becoming very popular and the proximity of Lyme with the health spa at Bath, encouraged hoards of visitors to the little seaside town. Like most tourists, they sought gifts to take home for their families and the fragments picked up by the Annings, which included pieces with such strange local names as 'Ladies Fingers' and 'Crocodiles Bones', proved ideal gifts as they lay displayed on a table outside Mr. Anning's shop.

The Anning saga then took a turn reminiscent of a Dickens' drama. Mr. Anning died of consumption – the prevalent disease of those times – and the mother, with Mary aged eleven and her fourteen year old brother, had to ask for Parish relief. To help their mother, the children continued to collect the fossils on the shore and sold them to visitors. They naturally met important collectors from geological societies, and became young celebrities in the collecting field. The more so when, in 1812, Mary found the skeleton of an 18 ft. long fish-like animal. Installed in a Museum of Natural History in London, it was later purchased by the British Museum and experts proclaimed it an Ichthyosaurus, a fish lizard, and said it was millions of years old.

Amongst the visitors who patronised the Anning collection was a Lt. Col. Birch of Thorpe Hall in Lincolnshire who, realising the family's poor circumstances, took the very generous step of selling his large fossil collection and giving the proceeds to the Annings.

From that time they never looked back and Mary's name as a collector became internationally famous. Without doubt, she must have had a lucky streak because further major discoveries occurred, including a flying reptile, Pterosaur, and the complete skeleton of a unique marine animal with a long neck which the experts called a Plesiosaurus. Over 30 ft. long, it was probably uncovered by the great storm of 1824 which destroyed the esplanade at Weymouth. In 1832 she uncovered another giant Ichthyosaurus, 30 ft. long, which can be seen in the Natural History Museum at Kensington, and later she again made the news when a cliff collapsed and she narrowly missed being buried alive – her little dog was killed.

It would be nice to relate that she grew up to become a kindly lady ever ready to help those who were interested in fossiling, and impart the great practical knowledge she had acquired over 30 years. She did become a personality but known for her bad temper and unfriendly nature. We must forgive her because she was suffering from a terminal disease, and it was a generous thought that prompted the Royal Geological Society in 1846 to create her an honorary member in recognition of her help to the world of geology. She did not live long to enjoy this new fame because 12 months later she died, and the Society further honoured her by installing a stained glass window in the parish church.

She could have been the Dorset town's most famous lady but, sadly, she is overshadowed by Jane Austen who chose Lyme as the location for her last great novel *Persuasion*. But the children who come in school parties each year to gather their sparkling 'Fool's Gold' and little curly 'Ammonites' will remember best Mary Anning, who pioneered a hobby that allows them to do the thing that little boys and girls like doing most – getting filthy on the ever moving shores of Pinhay Bay, and the towering grotesque cliff known as Black Ven. And who knows, one day one of them might even find a bigger Ichthyosaurus than Mary did.

11

Vaccination by Knitting Needle

TWO gravestones side by side in the churchyard of Worth Matravers, high in the Purbeck hills, commemorate a humble Dorset farmer and his wife who were laid to rest in the early years of the 19th century, and the puzzling and amusing inscription on one hints at an important event in the field of medicine.

Benjamin Jesty is the man who inoculated his wife and sons with cowpox serum, with the aid of a knitting needle, to prevent them catching the more serious disease of smallpox, and was rewarded by the Vaccine Pock Institute by them paying to have his portrait painted. That was his only reward for the sensational discovery. It would seem that his family, who were at the painful end of this experiment, suffered the risk of his crude 'needle' and did not even get a thank you from authority.

Farmer Jesty was farming at Yetminster in north Dorset in the 1770s and, being an observant man, he noticed that milkmaids seldom contracted the killing smallpox – the scourge of those times – but often suffered the much milder cowpox, which seemed to make them immune from the more serious disease. Taking the pus from diseased cows, he scratched the skin of his family with a knitting needle and rubbed the serum into the blood.

The Gloucestershire physician, Edward Jenner, gave up a promising career to experiment on the cure for smallpox, but it was many years after Jesty's experiment before he inoculated the arm of an eight year old boy with pus from a milkmaid's cowpox sore. Six weeks later the boy was again inoculated, this time with smallpox and it showed no reaction. It is believed that Jenner travelled in Dorset and had heard of Farmer Jesty's experiments, and of how he had protected his family from smallpox.

In 1798 Jenner published the results of his experiments, but he faced criticism and disbelief from the medical profession and had to campaign for years to get his cure accepted. However, it is Jenner who is credited with the discovery of vaccination and in 1802 a petition was put to the House of Commons, on Jenner's behalf, requesting he should be granted a reward for his achievement. In corroborative evidence, it was noted that others had carried out vaccinations and listed a Dorset farmer 'who had inoculated his wife and children.'

The Government decided that Jenner should have his reward – £10,000, in fact – because he had 'made the discovery of vaccination and given it liberally to the world'. Jesty's contribution was regarded as hardly relevant.

Dr. Andrew Bell, the vicar of Swanage, wrote to the Royal Jennerian Society reminding them of Jesty's earlier experiments and in 1805, the year of the battle of Trafalgar, the secretary of the Vaccine Pock Institute wrote to Jesty inviting him to come to London and stay not longer than five days for 'the purpose of taking your portrait as the earliest inoculator for cow pock'. He was promised fifteen guineas for his expenses.

The Institute also demanded their proof by inoculating Jesty and his sons with live smallpox serum to see if they were really immune, and issued a testimonial recording the 'remarkable vigorous health of Mr. Jesty's wife and two sons'. Mrs. Jesty reached the age of 84.

Farmer Jesty died on 16th April 1816 at the age of 79 and this is the inscription on his stone: 'He was born at Yetminster in this County and was an upright honest Man, particularly noted for having been the first Person (known) that introduced the Cow Pox by Inoculation, and who from his great strength of mind made the Experiment from the (Cow) on his Wife, and two Sons in the Year 1774.' Another stone in this lonely cemetery commemorates the death of Mary Brown who died in 1901, and states that her mother, Abigail, was personally inoculated for Cow Pox by Benjamin Jesty of Downshay, the first person known to have introduced the practice.

These sentences engraved in stone in this peaceful Purbeck cemetery tell the story of Benjamin Jesty and his important discovery.

Dr. Jenner petitioned Parliament again in 1806 and not only received another £20,000, but his birthplace at Berkely in Gloucestershire was bought for the nation as his memorial. There is no justice!

Perhaps we should be proud that the two men, both from Shire counties of England, became the leaders in the worldwide campaign of vaccination which has cleared the earth of the smallpox scourge.

12

Monmouth's Rebellion

THE Monmouth Rebellion in 1685, a fragment of English history, was an uprising lasting only 20 days and had its beginning and ending in Dorset. Like so many of the county's historical occasions, its scenario befits a swashbuckling film but without a happy ending.

The Duke of Monmouth was the result of a brief affair between Charles II and an Anglo-Welsh girl named Lucy Walter. She claimed that from her liaison with Prince Charles in Holland she gave birth to a boy on 9th April 1649. Charles recognised him as his son.

It was not much of a start in life for Monmouth. His 19 year old mother was described as 'a most beautiful strumpet' by a columnist of the day. When Lucy died at the age of 28, her child was passed to the care of a Royalist officer living in exile, and took the name of James Crofts.

By the time his father was restored to the Throne in 1660 to become Charles II, young James Crofts was thirteen. His grandmother, Charles I's widow, brought him to England and he became a favourite at Court. In 1663 the King conferred on him the title Duke of Monmouth and made him a Knight of the Garter, an honour that was later to become his downfall. He led a full life with countless mistresses.

He followed a distinguished military career, was brave and very popular with the ordinary people – leading several campaigns for the King. But he became too big for his boots and the King was not only very angry when Monmouth suggested himself as heir to the throne rather than the King's brother James, the Catholic Duke of York, but ordered him out of the country. There was, of course, intense hatred between Monmouth and the Duke of York. Monmouth went abroad to Holland with his favourite mistress, Henrietta Wentworth, with whom he was deeply in love.

However, a year later, in 1685, Charles II died suddenly and the Catholic James II came to the throne. The new King, fearing Monmouth's popularity, ordered a watch to be kept at all points lest Monmouth should come home. At the same time, the political faction of the Government who would have *anyone* as King as long as he was not a Catholic, persuaded Monmouth that he should come home and make a bid for the throne.

And this is why on 11th June 1685 three strange ships anchored off Lyme Regis – a frigate and two other vessels. Monmouth had arrived to commence his great campaign to claim the throne of England.

The ships were showing no colours and the very Loyalist Mayor of Lyme, Gregory Alford, sensing trouble and realising his own unpopularity in this port which had been a Roundhead stronghold in the Civil Wars, was very anxious.

Monmouth's party landed on the shingle just west of the Cobb and the occupants leapt ashore, some wading, others making secure the boats in the surf. A dominating tall figure dressed in a deep purple suit strode through the crowds and knelt in prayer. Slowly rising, he unfurled a flag and led the group towards town.

The townsfolk were soon aware that the leader was Monmouth and cheered him all the way to the marketplace calling 'A Monmouth! A Monmouth!'

News of Monmouth's arrival travelled fast. Entering the marketplace from Broad Street, the crowd collected around the black clad figure of Robert Ferguson, a former Presbyterian minister and one of the leaders of the revolt, who read the document of Declaration describing King James as 'the present usurper', amongst many other crimes. In a nearby field

Monmouth welcomed recruits as they queued beneath a large green flag emblazoned with the words 'Fear Nothing but God'. Over 90 signed up and were joined by 60 soldiers who had come ashore from the boats bringing arms and ammunition.

The next day training began. The tall men were drilled in the use of the heavy 16 foot pikes, and others were taught how to load and fire a musket.

He led his troops north recruiting as he journeyed through Axminster, Taunton, Bridgwater and Shepton Mallet, and then turned east into Wiltshire – an army of mostly untrained men, by this time over 1,000 strong, with about 150 horses bought and borrowed. They were literally going round in a circle and had no major town as a base. The King's men, moving in, captured Monmouth's ships in Lyme Bay, and on 26th June there was a clash at Norton St. Philip and Monmouth faced troops led by the Duke of Grafton, another of Charles II's illegitimate sons. The short and undecisive skirmish was called off because of torrential rain!

Monmouth's spirits were also dampened and he was giving up all hope of becoming King. There was no news of any men rallying to his cause in other parts of the country. Having come full circle, he passed through Shepton Mallet again and headed towards Sedgmoor where his campaign was to end. On the lonely peat moor in Somerset his untrained, inexperienced army was routed in a bloody battle on 6th July 1685.

His men lying slaughtered all around him, he left the field of battle accompanied by Lord Grey and a small party. He chose to aim for the New Forest where he could hide and await a boat for France. They galloped clear of the towns, spending a night at a friendly house, skirted the Dorset boundary and made for the Woodyates Inn, a few miles north of Cranborne on the Salisbury/Blandford road. As there was a reward of £5,000 on his head, Monmouth disguised himself as a shepherd. Discarding tired horses, his party split up for safety – all making for the coast, possibly Poole. Lord Grey was recognised and captured at Holt Lodge but Monmouth, exhausted, crawled into a ditch beneath a large ash tree near Horton to sleep. Next morning, a militia man, searching the fields, saw what he thought was an old coat and, beneath it, found the frightened figure of Monmouth. It was no use his protesting that he was a shepherd because in his pocket he had the gold insignia of the Order of the Garter, which identified him.

He pleaded for his life but James had no mercy. He threw him into the Tower and he was beheaded on 15th July. He faced death bravely, refusing to be blindfolded. The executioner made a botched job of the axing which a large crowd had gathered to watch. And so ended his doomed bid for the throne of England.

Little is left to remind us of his campaign, but the tree beneath which the exhausted Monmouth slept on his last night of freedom can be seen between two fields on Horton Common, near Peats Hill. A metal plate is affixed to its gnarled bark. It reads 'Monmouth Ash. After the Battle of Sedgmoor Duke of Monmouth lay hidden beneath this tree and was found and taken prisoner by William Portman and his militia. AD 1685.'

13

The Loss of the *Formidable*

THAT awesome expanse of English Channel, Lyme Bay, has claimed many naval vessels in its long history. Two submarines, the L24 and the aircraft-carrying M2 are rusting tombs sinking deeper into the sandy bottom of Hardy's Deadman's Bay. But the greatest disaster, in terms of human suffering, was the sinking of H.M.S. *Formidable* with the loss of 550 lives during the First World War, strangely enough sunk by a German submarine, with the familiar number U24.

On the last day of December 1914, *Formidable*, a battleship of 15,000 tons, with the rest of her squadron, took on mail and supplies at Plymouth. Less than 24 hours later she had joined thousands of other vessels as a tomb beneath the waves of the English Channel, not only a victim of a German U-boat's torpedo, but the first naval casualty of the war.

The Germans had developed their underwater fleet and it was a fearsome weapon in war against an island nation like Britain. In the first days of the war the presence of U-boats in the Channel brought the movement of shipping to a halt, and, as there was no means of detection, the submarines became a major menace.

British ships of the 5th and 6th Battle Squadrons were in the Channel to protect our supply lines. On this last day of 1914 Vice-Admiral Sir Lewis Bayly aboard the *Lord Nelson* led seven capital ships in line ahead. The *Formidable* was the last battleship followed by the light cruisers *Diamond* and *Topaze*. They had exercised all day and were returning to Portland.

New Year's Eve and the night began clear, with ships visible up to two miles. Through cloud gaps the moon illuminated the squadron and flecked the choppy sea. Midnight chimed and the crew could hardly have finished wishing each other a Happy New Year as the battleships sailed into Lyme Bay, when the enemy struck.

The German submarine U24 was nearing the end of an uneventful patrol in the Western Approaches, having left Wilhelmshaven before Christmas, and the Captain could not believe his luck as he saw smoke clouds from the squadron. Conditions were worsening, making it difficult for him to cruise at periscope depth so the U-boat boldly surfaced, came to within 100 metres of the *Formidable* and fired a torpedo into her amidships. *Formidable* shuddered and came out of the line, taking on a 20 degree list. So basic were communications that *Formidable's* captain did not know whether she had been torpedoed or had struck a mine. In spite of the cruisers circling the stricken battleship, the U24 fired a second torpedo and was so close that escaping she had to dive under the battleship, damaging her periscopes on the *Formidable's* keel. Captain Loxley went down with his ship and his old airedale dog, Bruce, was at his side on the bridge. The vessel settled, bow first, her stern still above water when the bow had touched the bottom. The violent storm which followed made rescue difficult and of the 780 men aboard 547 were lost.

One boat which got away grounded on the beach at Lyme Regis, 22 hours after the sinking. In the heaving seas, 14 men died of exposure and wounds and their bodies were pushed overboard. Of the 50 who landed, 9 were dead or dying. The dead were taken to the Pilot Beach Hotel and laid out on the floor. In the confusion, it was noticed that a crossbred collie, owned by the landlord, was licking the hands and face of one of the victims and lay across the man – thus warming the recumbent figure. The dog's odd behaviour attracted attention and Able Seaman John Cowan, a Scotsman, was found to be still alive. Dog and sailor became inseparable and it is claimed that the incident became the basis of the famous 'Lassie' stories.

There were many rumours regarding *Formidable*'s loss. It was said that the squadron steaming up Channel at a slow speed without an escort was a decoy to draw the attention of the U-boats and divert their presence from the ships transporting our troops across the Channel further east at Dover. England was rich in naval vessels and it was necessary to get troops ferried quickly across the Channel, unimpeded. The loss of a troop-ship by U-boat action would have been demoralising, so it was said that the vessels of the Naval Squadron were cruising openly up the Channel as 'sitting ducks', to draw U-boat fire, but this theory has been refuted.

Officially their Lordships at the Admiralty blamed Admiral Bayly, concluding their report, 'My Lords can form no other conclusion than that the handling of your squadron for the period in question was marked by want of prudence and good seamanship in avoidance of unnecessary risks inexplicable in an officer holding high and responsible command'. They would hear no explanation and ordered the Admiral to haul down his flag.

But there was a strange ending to this episode and it concerned Winston Churchill. Although Winston Churchill, First Lord, and Admiral Fisher, First Sea Lord, led the condemnation of Bayly, he was soon appointed to the important post of Commander-in-Chief, Western Approaches, and later in the war supervised 'Q' ship decoy operations from Cork, a command close to Churchill's heart.

Incidentally, Captain Loxley's old dog was washed ashore at Abbotsbury and is buried in Abbotsbury Churchyard.

14

Please can we have our Maces Back?

FEW local town councils can tell a tale of their past as bizarre and amusing as the strange situation which clouded the early part of the 19th century at Poole, when solicitor Robert Parr, the Town Clerk, unable to get his just rights from a Council nearing bankruptcy, sold not only the Council's furniture and the valuable town Maces but leased the Town Hall to a farmer for use as a store.

The intricate political 'goings-on' which led to this hilarious situation are told explicitly in *Ebbtide* written by another Town Clerk, John Hilliar, who continues to research Poole's history in his books published by the Poole Historical Trust.

Poole enjoyed a bonanza of trade posterity in the first few years of the 19th century. The Napoleonic Wars eliminated European competition in the supply of fish to sell in Europe, and preferential tariffs granted to the British merchants killed off American competition. In all the centuries of the Newfoundland trade, Poole merchants had never had it so good.

With the coming of peace in 1815, it all changed. Demand for fish fell off, the merchants lost their privileged position and Norwegian competition brought a shattering fall in the price of fish.

Earlier, Queen Elizabeth had made Poole a corporate and free town, by the title of 'the County of the Town of Poole' appointing its own Sheriff. The Corporation consisted of Mayor, four Aldermen and 28 Burgesses, and the right of electing Members of Parliament was lodged with them. Seventy-five men were listed in a directory as nobility, gentry and clergy and, as many of the gentry were the merchants, they had the most say in the way affairs were run – both nationally and locally.

Many influential citizens wanted to break the dominance of the Corporation and have some say in the election of Members of Parliament. They claimed they were the Commonalty but, in spite of the fact that they put up their own candidate on several occasions, the Sheriff disallowed their votes.

By 1821 those who sought Reform had sufficient support within the Tory dominated Corporation to get their views debated.

In 1826 the Reformers had the two Members of Parliament on their side. One, the Hon. W. F. S. Ponsonby, Lord of the Manor of Canford of which Poole was part, becoming the junior Member for Poole. Ponsonby, a Whig, who took his title through marriage, was the first Lord of the Manor to take an interest in governing for many years. It was he who financed and took up the cause of Reform in Poole, and it literally became a confrontation between the old Tory group which supported the Monarchy and the established order of the Church and State, and the Whigs' party which supported the superiority of Parliament over the Monarchy. A confrontation which was to prove to be bitter and against all the principles of modern government, without compromise.

The Reformers challenged the result of the first Municipal election as declared by the Tory Mayor. A select committee at the House of Commons inquired into the matter, declared it fraudulent and void and recommended an Act of Parliament to declare it void and to stage another election. Although this Poole Corporation Bill was passed by the House of Commons, the Lords threw it out.

Adding fuel to the worsening situation, the Lord of the Manor brought a suit at Chancery asking the court to declare as fraudulent the award which the former Tory Council had made to its ex Town Clerk in lieu of compensation, and the Reform magistrates refused to enforce any rates which might have allowed the Council to pay him.

Robert Parr, the Town Clerk, was not willing to wait and obtained a judgment of the Court of King's Bench which ordered the Council to pay. The Corporation were unable to pay, so the Court put Mr. Parr in possession of all the assets of the Corporation – its property, which included the church, town hall, marketplace and prison, as well as its 'personal property', the furniture in the Guildhall and its Maces. Mr. Parr received the rents of the Corporation's property and held an auction at which Council furniture and the valuable Maces were sold.

By this time, the Reformers were in power in the Council and immediately dismissed all the officers appointed by the Tories, including the new Town Clerk who seized the deeds and documents of the Corporation as a lien for his unpaid bills. Meanwhile Mr. Parr had taken over the Guildhall and let it to a farmer for £50 a year. The stately building, with its curved steps leading to the Tuscan pillared entrance – now the town's museum – became a hay store.

The proud and prosperous town of Poole, once the 'Metropolis of Newfoundland', was reduced to bankruptcy.

Through this long-running saga the reader has probably realised that Robert Parr, who was a wealthy man, had no real interest in reclaiming his dues but was revelling in the long litigation and the enjoyment it brought him. However, because of his whimsical sense of humour, it took Poole many years to round up and buy their Maces back.

A year later the furniture was retrieved for £46 1s 3d and the large Maces and ancient silver oar, symbol of the office of the Water Bailiff were sold back by Mr. Kemp Welch for £83 1s 6d. In fact it would seem that none of the property went far from home because 80 years later the exquisite William and Mary small Maces, bearing the Arms of the United Kingdom, and the town seals were bequeathed to the Corporation in 1931 in the will of J. Hayter Slade, a descendant of the Slades – merchants who played a prominent role in the tragic but amusing era in Poole's long history.

15

Free Love Portland Style

THE island of Portland, although moored to mainland Dorset by that pebble beach called Chesil, is inhabited by an insular populace who have always tried to divorce themselves from the people of the mainland. In the past – to use an old Dorset saying – 'They kept themselves to themselves', intermarrying and turning their backs on the outsiders who came to the island to open businesses.

The hard oolite rock lay just beneath the island's surface offering little help to those who would farm the land and, for the same reason, the island is practically treeless. The menfolk fished and reared the famous black-faced sheep, which ended up at many famous banquets as 'Portland mutton' and, in lesser social circles, the Portland mackerel were enjoyed.

The simple men of Portland found a new fame when Inigo Jones discovered that the stone of which the island is formed was excellent for building purposes. On the barren land hundreds of derricks sprung up like a forest as the men burrowed into their island and lifted out the blocks of grey-white stone which today graces many famous London buildings, including St. Paul's Cathedral.

However, the narrow way of life had created many strange superstitions. But the strangest and most ancient custom was the mode of taking a wife. At Portland, a local love custom existed whereby a young man could not marry his sweetheart until she became pregnant. This was, of course, an ancient practice but in the 19th century the country had adopted a more rigid Victorian moral code towards marriage and sex, and a girl getting pregnant before marriage brought all kinds of shame on herself and family – a situation to be hushed up. Not so in Portland where the hard life the men led fitted them to be in a condition to marry at an early age and start a family, and they were encouraged to choose their girls on the island. In such a small community an unproductive marriage was a wasted association, so the 'Portland custom' was adopted.

The girls did not admit to the attentions of a suitor but, on becoming pregnant, told their mothers who passed the information on to their fathers who told the boys it was time to marry.

If a girl did not conceive within a reasonable time of the courtship, the couple decided that they were not meant for each other and separated. They declared the affair 'broken off' and the girl, her honour in no way tarnished, sought another suitor and was accepted as a virgin.

Such was the integrity of the system that only one illegitimate child was recorded in the Parish Register in 150 years, but the inter-marrying and the mode of wife selection was productive of hundreds of stout and hardy children.

There was one slight hiccough. The growth of the quarrying trade drew workers from firms in London seeking the Portland stone. The first arrivals thought they had never had it so good, until some of the girls became pregnant and they were called upon to marry them. The men had not been advised regarding this part of the Portland custom and when they refused, the Portland women rose up to stone the men off the island. Those who did not take their sweethearts for better or worse, after such a fair trial run, were obliged to leave. This was the occasion when the lone bastard was born to upset the record books.

16

Studland's War Hero

THE old files of the *Dorset County Chronicle* revealed the intriguing story of Sergeant William Lawrence who fought bravely in most of Wellington's campaigns. He is buried in Studland churchyard and the life story of this incredible man and his French wife, buried with him, is told on a large tombstone. Sgt. Lawrence of the 40th Regiment of Foot saw a decade of active service against the French. In 1805 he was in South America fighting Spaniards, and in the Peninsular Wars he fought in most of Wellington's battles. He was a volunteer for the storming of Badajos, where he led a ladder party and was severely wounded but recovered to fight again at Waterloo. In the subsequent march to Paris he fell in love with a French girl, Clotilde Clairet as he camped at Germain-en-Loye, married her and brought her home to Studland where he kept an inn, appropriately called the Duke of Wellington – now known as the Bankes Arms to thousands of Purbeck walkers and, of course, considerably enlarged.

Lawrence was born in Briantspuddle in 1791 and, after an unhappy apprenticeship, ran away and joined the army. The next sixteen years were covered by his military career.

He could not write but, with the aid of a friend, produced an autobiography and in it describes how he met his wife as she served at a movable stall outside the camp which sold fruit, spirits, tobacco and snuff. His Colonel could not understand why he wanted to marry a French woman, but he was madly in love with her.

They eventually came to Studland after his discharge from the army, and he became a popular landlord because of his story telling. In *Old Swanage and Purbeck,* by William Masters Hardy, the author tells of Lawrence whom he knew. In 1847 alterations were being made to the old Manor House by the Hon. G. Bankes. Masters wrote: 'During the midday meal the men and boys would go down to the public house to partake of their meals and the ale which Mr. Bankes allowed each man and boy. The landlord was Waterloo veteran Sgt. Lawrence who had fought in the Peninsular Campaign and finally retired with several medals and ten clasps. Although one hour, the usual time, was allowed for dinner, sometimes it took an hour and a half to get through the meal, especially when the old soldier was in an anecdotal mood and related some of his thrilling and desperate adventures.'

One of his favourite yarns concerned the special boot polish the soldiers invented to make Wellington's boots shine. A long story which he retailed as well as his beer, it was a cunning ruse to keep his customers at the inn. The Lawrences lived in Studland for 38 years until the death of Clotilde.

After his wife died, he retired to a cottage in the village from which he was buried when he died in 1869.

He was given a full military funeral. The man who followed the Duke of Wellington through the Peninsular, fighting at Talavera, the man who fought at Vittoria and helped push the French back through the Pyrenees, was accorded the honour of a volley fired over his grave.

Studland is proud of its soldier hero, the man who self styled himself in a sub-title of his autobiography 'A hero of the Peninsular and Waterloo campaigns.'

17

Any More for the Skylark!

THERE have been Bolsons running small pleasure boats from Bournemouth beaches since John Henry Bolson, a fisherman from Alum Chine, obtained a licence to offer the public the *Queen* and *Amy Alice* in 1900. It was one of his sons, Jake, who not only gave the country the slogan 'Any more for the Skylark', became head of a shipbuilding empire – designing and building a purpose-built pleasure fleet – but emerged as a seafront 'character' known throughout the world. The strange and amusing extrovert is the subject of this Bournemouth saga.

Bournemouth-born Jake (Ginger) Bolson operated his first *Skylark*, a 13-seater motorboat, in the summer of 1914 but the War intervened and he served in the R.N.V.R. on minesweepers and did some Secret Service work.

When hostilities ceased, two *Skylarks* appeared on the Bournemouth scene ... Jake's original number one and a new 30-footer carrying 38 passengers, bought with his war gratuity. Two more boats swelled the fleet in 1921, one carrying 68 people, and in the following year Jake leased his first boatyard on Hamworthy Quay. 'The Skylark Shipyard' was base for building, repairing and overhauling Jake's growing *Skylark* Fleet as well as the repair of yachts and cruisers and commercial craft. By the mid-30s Jake Bolson owned a fleet which included *Skylarks, Larks, Titlarks* and *Speedlarks*, and his call 'Any more for the Skylark' echoed in the ears of thousands of Bournemouth holiday-makers.

Now you might imagine that a man in such a proud position,

with a son now established in the business as a designer and builder of boats, would have become a desk-bound executive. Not so Jake . . . to the end of his life on 27th June 1953 he never forsook his boats and the beach. David L. Chalk in his book *Any more for the Skylark* summed Jake up so well: 'His familiar figure in peaked yachting cap, jersey and rolled trousers were as much part of Bournemouth as the famous pine trees'.

Where do you begin to describe this man? Quick-tempered, with an acid wit yet basically shy with a heart of gold. I knew him for two years before I got a civil word out of him and it took many more years before I persuaded him to have his portrait taken aboard a *Skylark*. Once the barrier was broken down, I enjoyed many hours listening to his tales and philosophy.

It was his use of bad language that caused the most amusement. Sentences punctuated with oaths wherever he happened to be, yet he had a rare gift of being able to curse without causing offence. I once heard him deliver an angry admonishment to one of his boatmen during a Bournemouth Regatta. His swearing caused amusement throughout the passengers, including three nuns, who joined in the laughter. When he took on the role of Father Christmas and arrived at a Bournemouth store, landing from a *Skylark* at the Pier, some-one remarked 'Let's hope no-one offends him, or old Santa will take on a new image'. But this was the kind-hearted Jake, the same man who in 1936 flew the flags of the whole of his fleet at half-mast when his 12 year old Alsatian, Wolf, died. The dog was his constant companion on the beach, guarding the pay-box, and was a favourite with visitors. His wickedness came to the fore one afternoon. I was talking to him when two dear old ladies approached. 'My man', started one of the ladies pompously, 'where do we get tickets for the Isle of Wight trip?'. Straight-faced, he questioned 'Have you got yer bloody passports?'. 'Oh, no', replied the lady in surprise. He sent them off through the Gardens to the Town Hall where he told them they could be obtained. When I remarked that his action was unkind, he replied with a wry smile: 'They ought to have more bloody sense'.

In 1952 he instituted a Bolson Fleet Regatta for his boatmen, held at a time when most visitors were at tea. One of the events was a race, in identical rowing boats, to the sewer buoy and back. 'What about the old man?', I enquired, seeing a veteran who must have been nearly 70. 'Is he not going to have a start?' 'No', said Jake with an oath . . . 'the old bugger gets the choice of boats.'

Jake had his own views on the Poole claim that the bay at Bournemouth was Poole bay. 'Look', he said, indicating the beaches to the right and left of him. 'Between Hengistbury Head and Sandbanks there are seven miles of glorious sand, along Bournemouth beaches. Down there', he said indicating the entrance to Poole Harbour three miles away, 'is a bloody great creek and Poole is five miles up it. How can it be Poole Bay?'

This fair-skinned, ginger-haired character, his lips constantly chapped with long exposure to the sun and who only put on his shoes on Monday lunchtime to attend Rotary, passed away in 1953 in a house overlooking the Pleasure Gardens. The house where he once raged in temper when a journalist called to report on his rumoured death during a typhoid scare. A house with a steering wheel built into its gate, bearing the name *Skylark's Nest.*

18

All for Love

THE classic love story of Robert Browning and Elizabeth Barrett is etched on the hearts of poetry lovers, and another with a similar romance was Dorset dialect poet, William Barnes.

Born in 1801, he passed a pleasant childhood as he played by the sleepy River Stour and cast stones into the placid waters at Cut Mill near his birthplace at Bagber in the Blackmoor Vale, and walked to school at Sturminster Newton two miles to the south.

At 18 years of age, he left home for Dorchester to become an engrossing clerk to a firm of solicitors.

William Barnes was an artistic dreamer and preferred practising the arts of woodcut and copperplate engraving, spending hours with sketchbook in hand in the High Street of the county town. One day his reverie was disturbed by the clattering of a stagecoach as it drew up at the Kings Arms Hotel. As the restless horses stood steaming after their journey, William watched a family alight from the upper deck. His eyes feasted on a young 16 year old girl, with beautiful blue eyes, brown hair and a warming smile. Transfixed, he vowed there and then that she should be his wife. Julia, the youngest daughter of James Canfield Miles, had arrived in his life.

Wishes are easy; turning his wishes into reality was to prove more troublesome. Mr. Miles was a stern Supervisor of Excise, arriving to take up his post at Dorchester. The young dreamer

Barnes, with no known prospects of a reasonable job, definitely did not appeal to him as a future son-in-law.

William wooed his Julia on the banks of the river Frome where it twists through the meadows behind Dorchester and, although he was making a name for himself as an engraver, he was making no impression on Mr. Miles.

To improve his prospects, in 1823 Barnes took a post as schoolmaster at a school in Mere, a sleepy town just over the county's north border. There he worked hard for four years to earn enough to give him the right to ask for Julia's hand in marriage.

Absence made William's heart grow fonder and, while at the Chantry House School, he composed some of his loveliest sonnets.

> 'A sweet secluded garden! charming sound
> To those who seldom seek the world like me.
> Secluded be it so that none may see
> Within the woody boundaries around
> And while the songs of warbling birds resound,
> And while I hear the humming of the bee
> Around the growing fruit upon the tree,
> And flowers of every colour on the ground.
> There, blithely busied, I will toil to store
> My ripened crops, until the chilly days
> Of early darkness, and of glowing fires.
> And when the hollow winds of winter roar,
> I'll sit me down beside the cheerful blaze
> In happiness. To this my soul aspires.'

William Barnes eventually married his Julia in 1827. He took his bride home to Mere and wrote in his diary 'On a happy day – happy as the first of a most happy wedded life – I brought into it Julia Miles bespoken by an early choice than which I cannot conceive a better.' Julia bore him six children and when she died 25 years later he was distraught. He wrote in his misery –

'My Julia, my dearest bride,
Since thou has left my lonely side,
My life has lost its hope and zest,
The sun rolls on from east to west,
But brings no more that evening rest,
Thy loving kindness made so sweet,
And time is slow that once was fleet,
As day by day was waning.'

As time passed he wrote more objectively of his sorrow and, reverting again to dialect verse, he transferred his own experience to a poor Dorset countryman and produced the moving *Wife A' Lost*, of which the last verse goes:

'Since I do miss your vaice an feace
In prayer at eventide,
I'll pray wi' woone said vaice vor greace
To goo where you do bide;
Above the tree an' bough, my love,
Where you be gone avore,
An' be a waiten vor me now,
To come vor evermore.'

William never recovered from the loss of his Julia and he wrote her name in his diary every day until the end of his life.

19

Mine Host of Swanage

MR. William Hixson could hardly be called a jovial Mine Host. In the middle of the 19th century, he ran the Royal Victoria Hotel at Swanage. The town's number one hostelry earned its name because the great Queen Victoria had stayed there when she was a Princess in 1833.

In the year 1856, two gentlemen and a boy arrived at the hotel and, after lunch, told the proprietor that they wished to stay the night and would require three beds. Surly Mr. Hixson bluntly told them that the hotel was very busy, and he could only let them have two beds. 'The young gentleman will have to sleep on a sofa, that is the best I can do', he said. The gentlemen registered their displeasure but Mr. Hixson then became very cross and told them they would have to try elsewhere if they were not satisfied. They conferred and decided that, as the stay was only for one night, they would make do with the arrangements.

One of Mr. Hixson's pet aversions was inquisitive young boys, so he did not take kindly to a request from the young guest when he asked to look around the ballroom. 'I have no time to show boys around', he said in a surly manner, and became quite angry when the boy said he would also like to see the room in which the Queen had slept 23 years earlier.

The next morning after breakfast, the party packed their bags and left. They then spent the day wandering along the beautiful clifftops of Dancing Ledge to St. Aldhelm's Head.

The young 'gentleman' was none other than H.R.H. Edward,

Prince of Wales, travelling incognito on an educational trip to the south coast. At the young prince's request the group walked along the rugged cliff path to St. Aldhelm's Head, marked out with white washed stones as a guide to coastguards patrolling at night. They chose 7½ miles of the choicest scenery to be enjoyed on the south coast. It included the comparatively new giant globe of the world at Durlston and Tilly Whim Caves. He was most interested in the ancient signal house erected during the Napoleonic wars on Round Down above the cliffs, and the antiquated lowering machinery consisting of windlass and gibbet used by quarrymen to lower the blocks of Purbeck stone on to barges.

Mr. Hixson had probably forgotten all about them until the day came when the account was settled. Opening his post, Mr. Hixson found the payment which bore the signature of H.R.H. The Prince of Wales.

Shocked, he was overawed that he had not only entertained royalty unawares, but that it had been none other than the future King of England. He was vexed and mortified as he remembered that he had given him anything but a royal reception.

It is said that he stamped and swore and then vowed that he would never behave in such a manner again, but would be kind and civil to all his customers – rich and poor alike.

They dared not tell the demented Mr. Hixson that the young prince, travelling incognito, had been told by his mother – by this time Queen of England – to ask to see the ballroom and rooms she had resided in during her own visit to Swanage.

20

Gulliver: King of Smugglers

IT is sad that the powerful and outspoken conservationists who successfully save Victorian buildings today in Bournemouth were not operating in the 1950s, when a disgusting act of official vandalism was embarked upon at Kinson. Developers tore down the former home of Isaac Gulliver, undisputed King of the south's smugglers. It was a purpose built house, complete with tunnels and secret rooms. Had it been saved and made into a museum of 18th century smuggling, it would have become a leading tourist attraction.

The rambling house had crenellations giving it the appearance of a fortress. In spite of its attractive outward appearance, Gulliver's requirements for the interior must have been a nightmare to the architect. There were ingenious secret cupboards and passages and, ten feet up the chimney place, was a door to a large secret room. Carpet covered a trapdoor in the dining room giving access to a cellar from which tunnels led away from the house. One is said to have led the three miles to Branksome, but I believe the tunnels linked up with other Kinson houses.

Pompous Bournemouth proudly boasts of her associations with Squire Tregonwell, the Shelleys and a variety of authors but, almost in shame, it disassociates itself from its most colourful character ... the entrepreneur, farmer, landowner, publican and smuggler-in-chief who truthfully could have claimed 'By Royal Appointment' on his letterhead. Isaac Gulliver was a legend in his own lifetime.

Although his infamous trading was centred around Bournemouth, he was not a Dorset man but was born near Melksham in neighbouring Wiltshire in 1745. At an early age he displayed his flair for leadership. He became a giant of a man, not only brave but with a keen financial ability. Most dominant of all was his sense of humour, which coloured activities as his great smuggling empire spread westward almost to Cornwall. Son of a smuggler, he married at the age of 23. His bride, Elizabeth Beale, was a Dorset lass whose father was the landlord of the Blacksmiths Arms on the main Salisbury to Blandford road.

Taking over the inn, he immediately changed the name – probably tongue in cheek – to the Kings Arms, to show, he said, his loyalty to the Crown. He moved to Longham in Dorset to become landlord of the White Hart, a centre only a few miles from Bournemouth and Branksome beaches where his fleet of 15 luggers could land their contraband. The now vast conurbation of Bournemouth and Branksome was then a Great Heath with few houses in sight, and the smugglers' paths can still be traced from the chines and beaches across remaining heathland to Kinson.

By 1776 Gulliver had a team of 50 well trained smugglers whose quaint uniform was the smock of the style worn by Dorset shepherds. Their hair was long, tied into a knot and powdered. Gulliver had made friends in high places, often by bribery, and the uniform made them recognizable as Gulliver's men and gave them protection. They were known as the White Wigs and Gulliver himself earned the title of 'The Gentle Smuggler' and boasted that he never killed a King's man – his only weapon being a small pistol.

Gulliver had many battles with his arch enemy, Abraham Pike, the King's Riding Officer from Christchurch, and these were the basis of some of the amusing yarns told of the smuggler.

Setting out ahead of his gang from Bournemouth beach on one occasion, he galloped off carrying a keg of brandy, through the woods out on to the Great Heath. At a crossroads, Abraham

Pike called out a challenge in the King's name. Spurring his white horse and with knowledge of the paths, Gulliver got home ahead of his pursuers. The stable boy quickly turned the horse out into the paddock and Gulliver raced indoors and disappeared beneath the dining room.

Mrs. Gulliver, a great asset to her husband, was used to covering up in emergencies and quietly went on with her knitting. As Pike knocked on the door, she suddenly saw the brandy keg on the floor. Without panicking, she put a cushion over it and – using it as a footstool – covered the keg with her voluminous skirts. As Pike was shown into the room she said calmly: 'I'm afraid Mr. Gulliver is not at home.' Frustrated, Pike stormed out saying he would return next day with a search warrant. He duly arrived pompously to be met by a tearful household. 'Gulliver is dead,' they said and took Pike to see the smuggler chief in a coffin, his eyelids closed and his face whitened.

Pike was taken aback, spluttered his condolences and removed his hat in respect. The news of Gulliver's death had spread around the village, so a funeral was arranged – the vicar being fooled – and a stone-filled coffin was buried. Gulliver had to spend a few months in another part of his realm, probably at his farm at Eggardon Hill in West Dorset.

He was once nearly captured in Poole – a port with a large staff of customs men. When he was spotted, he fled to an inn which had a friendly landlord. Isaac was bundled into a large empty cask which was lifted onto a waiting wagon outside. He was carried through the streets and out of town, right under the noses of the King's men.

As he grew older, he gave up his smuggling activities and announced in the important *Gentleman's Magazine* that he would concentrate on selling fine wines and spirits to the gentry. He hoped for 'continued favours of friends and customers'. This amusing statement fooled no one, least of all his arch enemy, Abraham Pike. Once, when nearly caught making a transaction at Wimborne, he quickly borrowed an old smock and mingled with the market crowd disguised as a farmhand.

Pike had little chance against this man who once sold smuggled goods to the Royal household at Weymouth and earned the thanks of the King himself when he warned him of a plot on his life. 'Let Gulliver smuggle as he will,' said a thankful Monarch. Pike's determination resembled a 'baddy' in a television series who seems to be winning in every episode but always loses out at the end.

The prosperous Gulliver retired to Wimborne in 1817, proving again that dishonesty does pay because he left a fortune running into several million pounds in modern currency. His novel-sized will of 12,000 words disclosed that he owned property in four counties, but there was something of a Robin Hood about him and he endowed numerous charities. He died on 13th September 1822, aged 77 years, an unlucky Friday. He was mourned by men from every walk of life from Squire to simple farmhand, because he sold quality goods at reasonable prices.

How does Bournemouth remember this colourful character? His only weapon – a tiny lady's reticule pistol – has a corner in a glass case in the Russell Cotes Museum. There could have been his house too. But one morning in 1958 the dust rose as workmen tore down the magnificent staircase from West Howe Lodge – Gulliver's home. It could have become an international shrine to the 'Gentlemen of the Night' who, unlike today's purveyors of drugs, smuggled only the good things of life ... brandy, silks, yes and even tea.

21

The Man who Bought Kisses

BOURNEMOUTH has had more than its share of eccentrics – those larger-than-life characters whose exploits creep into conversation when the town is discussed far afield. Chang, the Chinese giant; the tall elegant lady who wore ankle-length coats and daily fed the squirrels; the man who stood in front of the band in the Pleasure Gardens and conducted with his walking stick. And then there was Cumberland Clark, an elderly, immaculate and wealthy 'man-about-town', who was exceedingly handsome and very aware of it.

Mr. Clark was a prolific author who wrote on subjects which ranged from *Dickens and his Jewish Characters* to *England's Fight against Communism*, not forgetting his fairy plays for children, poetry and the *Bournemouth Song Book.* His poetry was a disaster, yet a comprehensive and amusing commentary on Bournemouth and district in those halcyon pre-war days.

> 'The English coast can proudly boast
> Of many beauty spots;
> Of sands and bays for holidays
> We happily have lots.
> But yet to me 'twould ever seem
> When I of their allurements dream
> That lovely Bournemouth reigns supreme.'

The opening verse of *Beautiful Bournemouth* gives a clue to what is meant. Other towns in the area get similar treatment, even sedate Beaulieu:

'If I ever went to Bournemouth I should think my conduct shabby
Should I come away without a stay at Beaulieu Abbey.
You really find it doesn't take a deal of time to get there,
And a lot of things of interest are always to be met there.
If you want the church to see, you will find you go in free
And must enter with a reverence of manner.
But it breaks the Scotsmen's hearts when they visit other parts
For they find the admission is a "tanner".'

Over 130 such epics deal with the pines, the hotels, stores, Bournemouth amusements and, of course, yachting:

'When at Bournemouth, if you've got
A notion you would like a yacht
And your cash is quite a lot
Go and buy one on the spot.
Folks will point and say "Big Pot!
Simply tons of money, what?
A millionaire he is. Great Scot!"
And all that kind of tommy rot.'

Whatever his reputation as a poet, Cumberland Clark had another reputation that he certainly delighted in. He was fond of the ladies!

He could be observed most mornings standing on the corner of Richmond Hill near the Norfolk Hotel, admiring the girls on their way to work.

For each he had a smile, but some made a deeper impression. Cumberland had snow-white hair combed into a neat quiff, and a well-groomed white walrus moustache curled at the ends and, when his interest was really stirred, he tweaked his moustache and rocked from one foot to another. Sometimes, after a conversation, he would lead a young lady off to his flat nearby and it is said that he was known to offer girls half-a-crown for an innocent kiss. It is also said that restaurant waitresses fought to wait on his table because if they gave a little extra attention, he would give them a big tip.

However, the philandering and penmanship of Cumberland Clark ended in a night of violence which was not of his making. In January 1941, a stray enemy bomb demolished the block of flats in Central Bournemouth where he lived, and he perished among the rubble and the scattered manuscripts of his life's work.

His admirers held an annual dinner in his memory up until the 1970s, by which time numbers had sadly diminished. But they did once insert a notice in *The Times* 'In Memoriam' column which amusingly if rather misleadingly read: 'Cumberland Clark, killed by enemy action 1941.'

22

The Brave Lifeboatmen

LIFEBOATMEN'S heroism is reflected in the image of open red, white and blue lifeboats cresting giant waves as they approached disabled wallowing windjammers with their sails in ribbons – a subject popular with Victorian artists. The bravery of such life-saving fishermen clad in cumbersome cork life-jackets and yellow sou'westers fills books, and provides a lengthy roll of honour. Many of these lifeboats ended as debris on the rugged rocks around our shores and the crews were never to be seen again.

Dorset, with its seaboard extending along the Channel shore, has played many a leading role in dramatic sea rescues, and an incident of extreme courage is recorded in the annals of the Swanage Station. In 1890, 36 years after the R.N.L.I. had been formed, a new boat was allotted to Swanage where they had to be launched by slipway – often into the full force of easterly gales. The 37 feet, 12 oared *William Erle* was the latest design in rescue boats but the crew were convinced that she lacked stability, and three years later she was replaced without having made a single service call.

In 1893 a new *William Erle* arrived. On paper it would seem very little different from the discarded craft. Both were self-righting, and the same length, and both were just over 4 tons in weight. The only major difference, not to be seen with the naked eye, was one foot extra on the new boat's beam measurement. She measured 9 feet and, at £584, cost £51 more than her predecessor. (Today a lifeboat can cost well over £150,000.)

Whatever the merits of the new *William Erle* the crew had faith in her but two years later, on the first service call, their belief was badly shaken.

During the afternoon of 12th January 1895, the Norwegian Barque *Brilliant* got into difficulties off the Hook Sands at the entrance to Poole Harbour. The *William Erle* sped down the slipway into the worst possible type of sea the Swanage boat had to face. The wind, south-east by east, swept into the bay at gale force with frequent blinding flurries of snow. Coxswain William Brown yelled encouragement as his 12 oarsmen headed into the teeth of the storm. He was pleased with the progress but, arriving off Old Harry Rocks, they ran into a confused sea. The ebbing tide racing out of Poole against the wind sent the seas in turmoil as the water swept over the ledges. A series of high waves came up on the lifeboat's quarter and she broached-to. The boat stood it well and quickly recovered without capsizing but the sea had washed both crew and gear from end to end, and two had gone overboard. Thomas Marsh was nearby and quickly hauled back. The crew saw William Brown drifting away and made superhuman efforts to get the oars sorted and head to their Coxswain's aid. In the turmoil their task was impossible and they could get no help from the sail because of damage to the foremast.

Both crew and boat were now in danger of running ashore beneath the towering white cliffs of Ballard and the crew gazed anxiously seawards, but brave Coxswain Brown had disappeared in the raging water, lost in the constant swirl of wave and foam. In the interests of the crew and damaged vessel, the second Coxswain had to make the hardest and most heartrending decision of his life – he had to leave his chief and limp back to Swanage.

In the best tradition of the Service, the RNLI did not let the Barque down. The *Brilliant*, laden with cedar logs from Nuevitas in Cuba, eventually grounded on the Hook Sands, at Poole. The gale was now blowing a full Force 10 and whipping up the snow. The small lifeboat *Boy's Own No. 2*, operating from

Poole, went to her rescue in the darkness. The ten-oared boat was towed out of port by the old steam tug *Telegraph* a wooden-hulled paddleboat. She slipped her tow on the seaward side of the stricken vessel and the lifeboat oarsmen manoeuvred magnificently, running downwind, and snatched the whole crew of ten from death. They took off one man at a time as it was too rough for the lifeboat to tie up alongside the stricken *Brilliant*. The Captain, who had sustained a broken rib earlier, slipped into the water during the rescue, but the lifeboat crew quickly recovered him. The ship's boy sustained a broken leg when his limb became entangled in wet ropes, but quick thinking by the Poole crew saved the boy's leg by hacking through the ropes with a knife. By this time a blinding snowstorm made rescue the more difficult and, with the last man safely aboard the lifeboat, the crew picked up the *Telegraph*'s tow rope and made themselves reasonably comfortable with sails folded to make a shelter, until they reached the lee of the Poole Haven Point.

23

Tragedy at Sherborne

IT is difficult to associate a degrading sexually orientated murder with the peaceful abbey town of Sherborne, which clings to Dorset where the border meets Somerset. Just as this little town lying in the valley of the river Yeo, at the foot of a green slope, was preparing to celebrate the festival of Christmas in 1935, and shops were aglow with Christmas lights illuminating the lush food offerings, tragedy struck and Sherborne received a sickening shock that was to haunt it for a long time.

The mysterious death of Fred Bryant, a cowhand from nearby Nether Compton, started a murder hunt that eventually led his wife to the scaffold at Exeter prison. A long police enquiry and court case unravelled a foul murder of the type national newspapers revelled in publishing in the 1930s.

The ladies of Sherborne became aware of Charlotte Bryant, alias 'Compton Liz' or 'Black Bess' who had been in their midst – a woman living in poverty with her husband who sought escape in her local pub, accepting drinks from men and afterwards taking them home to her cottage. These liaisons were not only pleasurable but enabled her to supplement the 30 shillings a week earned by her husband. Her illicit affairs were lucrative and enabled her to lead a better lifestyle.

This woman of Irish/Gypsy origin was not even attractive. Her Counsel said at the trial 'she lacked beauty, dignity, charm or any other attraction'. Fred Bryant had married her when he was serving in the Army during the Irish troubles of 1922. She was 19 years of age at that time and thought her young soldier in uniform would take her away from a life of poverty. The dream soon faded when she saw him in his civilian role, earning such a meagre wage. She had literally exchanged one poverty for another in England. In fairness it must be said that her husband was aware of her affairs and condoned them, knowing the extra money was useful. She became cunning and devised ways of extracting money from her men friends. A businessman from Yeovil who thought she was carrying his child handed her £25 to pay for an abortion. Later she turned up with the baby demanding regular payments for her silence. Neither the businessman nor Fred Bryant were the baby's true father.

She met her most serious lover, a travelling horse dealer with a gypsy background, in 1933. He was the father of her fifth and last child. He not only came to live with the Bryants, but became a friend of the husband.

Early in 1935, Fred Bryant suffered the first of what was to become a series of mysterious illnesses from which he eventually died, and for which his wife was tried and hanged. Fred Bryant was poisoned over a long period of time.

The murder trial itself, in which young children were brought into court to give evidence, had a shattering effect on this peaceful Dorset town. Sherborne was a typical English market town of charm, dominated by its great Abbey around which it literally nestled. It lingered in the past and resembled a permanent film set for Trollope novels. You could almost expect to meet the Rev. Septimus Harding, Mr. Quiverful or Bishop Proudie in the short passage which lead from the Conduit in the main street to the Abbey.

Houses of charm lined the narrow streets. Timber-faced dwellings with overhanging upper storeys, homes with stone mullioned casements from Tudor days and even Georgian bow-fronts in red brick had given over their lower floors to shopkeeping; very elegant little businesses selling antiques, expensive ladies underwear and gentlemen's shops where clothes were predominantly county and for the hunting field. The people sounded very county and only in public bars did you pick up fragments of the rich Dorset dialect.

It was a quiet town, free of scandals where most people you passed in the street were probably something in the church, or at least a member, where street conversations were whispered as if the whole town was part of the Abbey precinct.

The residents had to endure the posse of crime reporters who encamped at Sherborne throughout the time the sordid crime unravelled, and the comings and goings of Scotland Yard's bowler-hatted Chief Inspector Alec Bell and Detective Sergeant Tapsell and their entourage who led the investigation. The daily events made front page news for many weeks. It was said that some local men were biting their finger nails as the investigation progressed and some wives checked their husband's movements over the previous year or two. Sherborne suffered. Its calm had been disturbed and each daily headline added to the shame.

The case was controversial right until the hour of Charlotte Bryant's death, and after. The sad fact is that the Sherborne affair ended with two people dead and five children orphaned.

In her last desperate act Charlotte sent a telegram to King Edward VIII. It said 'Mighty King have pity on your lowly afflicted subject. Don't let them kill me on Wednesday', but she was hanged on 15th July 1936 and Sherborne slipped from the headlines and returned to the simple role of entertaining tourists. Today the murder is almost forgotten and you will find few who remember it, and even fewer who wish to talk about it.

24

The Pirates of Poole Harbour

MEN of Poole are not usually the jolliest of characters. Maybe the reason dates back to the plight of their ancestors who lived in fear because they were constantly chased through the streets by marauding Danes. But they do let their hair down at the periodical ceremony of Beating the Bounds of the Harbour. This ancient and unique occasion confirms the fishing boundaries of Poole as laid down in a Charter granted by the Barons of Winchester in 1364 ... basically to put an end to the quarrelling between the burgesses of Poole and Wareham over fishing limits, and to define a boundary across Wareham Channel. At the harbour entrance the seaward limits were measured by floating a large Humber barrel on the ebbing tide until it disappeared from the view of observers.

With pride the men of Poole made their first ceremonial beating of the bounds in 1612 – a dignified event, with the Mayor and Magistrates in a boat festooned with flags and accompanied by townsfolk in other craft. 'The vessels moved along to the tune of music on board and an air of happy interest prevailed.'

The ceremony has never been ruled by a set historical programme. Through the centuries successive organisers have changed the rules to suit their time, so while in 1631 it was a religious occasion with the trooping of the colours and a visit to church to 'give glory to God', in 1649 the humorous leg-puller, Richard Bramble, was Town Clerk and he turned the proceedings into a pleasure which was described as 'rough and crude'.

The Mayor and menfolk rowed down to North Haven at the harbour entrance where the Mistress Mayoress and ladies from the town awaited them. 'After having erected a tent with the oars and sails of the boat, we refreshed ourselves with such victualls as God had provided for the perambulation and the young men disported themselves with their hats playing a kind of football.'

From this official account of the proceedings, I fear that the men had already had a fair share of God's victualls on the journey down the harbour.

After the Mayor had made his proclamation and read the Charter for all to hear, it pleased Mr. Moses Durell to take two young men by the hand and 'lead them knee deep in the ocean' and then march them back again. My fears were affirmed and when the ale had run out and the men were tired of playing football, they caught the flowing tide for a quick passage to Poole Quay. This was a long time before the days of women's equal rights, and I again quote the official record:

'At the quay the women departing to their several habitations (after salutations past), Mr. Mayor with the rest of the Magistrates and men in his company went to Mr. Melmoth's inn, where having for a little while refreshed themselves with some wine, beer and tobacco everyman taking his leave one of the other in a civil, loving and courteous manner, they departed to their respective homes, without any observation of any remarkable incivility through the passage of the day.' One wonders how they could stand up.

There were several perambulations in the 18th and early 19th centuries and then it died out for 100 years to be revived in 1921. Early in these modern day celebrations there occurred an incident which shaped the pattern of 20th century Bounds Beating escapades.

The Mayor, who is also Admiral of the Port of Poole sent out the invitations for a harbour perambulation but certain businessmen were omitted from the list. Angered, they decided to hire a boat and, dressed as pirates, set out to mar the dignity of the event and make a nuisance of themselves by douching the Admiral's Barge with water.

Pirate intervention became a leading spectacle in future events, and the capture of the pirates at the end of the day preceded sentencing, when they were forced to walk the plank into the harbour – to the delight of visitors who lined the quayside. The serious happenings in the ceremony included the reading of the Charter in the presence of the jury at all the boundary marks around the vast harbour. At each stop schoolgirls had their fingers pricked with a celebration pin so that they remembered the day. Schoolboys were left with a more undignified memory – their bottoms were smote with a leather thong.

Shopkeepers dreaded the arrival of the pirates on the morning of the event, wondering if they were scheduled for particular attention. Once, the pirates took over a hairdressing salon, commandeering the hairdryers while angry customers gathered tightlipped in their hair nets and curlers. They then proceeded to carry all the barmaids from the inns chaining them to the lamp posts, and then forcing the sullen landlords to serve the ale.

By the end of the 1970s the ceremony had developed into a water carnival with an old time fayre on the quayside, complete with roundabouts and sideshows. The day ended with a great waterborne procession from Sandbanks to Poole Quay. . . . The Admiral's Barge, the jurymen dressed in the garb of Nelson's day sailors aboard Royal Marine landing craft, pirate vessels flying the Jolly Roger abreast of police and coastguard launches, lifeboats, fishing boats and an armada of yachts all heading into the sinking red sun as it lowered behind the glowering Purbeck Hills, a colourful finale with the Admiral's Barge at its head.

Of all the amusing incidents that have coloured the Bounds Beating ceremony, the storming of Brownsea Island in 1947 and confrontation with the famous recluse, Mrs. Bonham Christie, was a historical highlight.

The lady, who lived almost alone in the great mansion on

Brownsea, followed a succession of unusual characters who have owned the island, which stands at the entrance to Poole Harbour. Few people knew what she looked like because she was seldom seen and made only rare visits to the mainland. They formed opinions of a fearsome lady from the reports in the press of her treatment of any who tried to land on her island. She employed a Scandinavian woman of Amazon proportions who physically threw trespassers off the island. An engineer handyman completed the island's population and the wildlife, including peacocks and the rare red squirrels, lived in peace. The only strangers allowed on the island were members of the Boy Scout Movement, so that they could visit the site on the far side of the island where Baden Powell had set up his first camp soon after the turn of the century. Even when fire raged across the island in the early 1930s, reducing it to a blackened mass of ash and a forest of naked tree stumps, Mrs. Christie was reluctant to have firefighters 'landing on her kingdom'. It took many years for those scars to heal.

I must confess that I joined the pirate gang hoping to persuade them to call on the recluse so that I could meet her, and on a sunny afternoon in 1947, with much shouting and yelling, we headed the pirate galleon for Brownsea's landing quay, stormed ashore and knocked on the door of the great mansion. Faint footsteps grew louder and noisy bolts were drawn. Then, the massive door opened slowly and squeakily as in a horror film, and a dear little old lady in a woolly jumper with a scarf wrapped around her pale, smiling face, restraining the silver hair, inquired of our business. To say the least, we were taken aback – having prepared for a verbal confrontation and a demand that we leave at once. At once we warmed to this dear old lady who could have been anyone's favourite granny. We were speechless and pushed the pirate chief to the fore. Now, ship's chandler Steve Colombos was no taller than Mrs. Christie and he looked an amusing figure in his floppy hat and Wellington boots which, because of his diminutive stature, reached up to his knees – rather like Paddington Bear.

Overawed by her presence, and doffing his hat in respect, he stuttered 'M ... Ma ... Mam, my friend here wants to take yer photee.' The legendary lady gave him a warm smile and came out on to the quayside and posed with the pirate gang, put a note in their collecting box and told them to call again next time.

25

The Sad Princess of Critchel

CRITCHEL House today stands proudly reflecting itself in a 30 acre lake – without doubt one of the loveliest houses in Dorset. After the destruction of the village by fire in 1742, the remains were flattened and the new house was planned so that it could enjoy a sylvan setting amongst terraced gardens backed by green slopes.

It is sad that such a beautiful house was once the unhappy 'prison' of a young English princess. Had she survived her unhappy early life and become Queen she would have changed the course of our history.

The great house with its pillared portico is reached by climbing a charming curved flight of steps. Many master builders of the day had a hand in its design – in the style of Robert Adam. James Wyatt was responsible for the dining room. There are medallions on the walls and, framed in the frieze of the chimney piece, is a painting by Sir Joshua Reynolds of a group of boys. The drawing room is even more elaborate, with a Venetian window whose round arch rises above lovely marble columns flanked by side windows. It made a strange prison for a princess.

When the future George IV was persecuting his wife, Queen Caroline, he took away their only child, Princess Charlotte, and sent her to More Critchel with orders that she should not be allowed to see her mother.

The Prince of Wales and Caroline of Brunswick separated when Charlotte was still in the cradle and she was brought up by governesses. She grew up at More Critchel but few people were concerned with the situation of a girl who might one day be Queen, because the news of the time centred around England's attempts to defeat Napoleon.

The unhappiness which marred her parents' lives did not spoil the young girl and she is said to have had a charming disposition. At 17 years of age she became formally engaged to the young Prince of Orange, but because of an intense love for her own country she would not return to Holland with him and broke the engagement off.

Her father was furious and dismissed all her household. Charlotte fled to her mother but got no sympathy there and was eventually sent to live alone in Cranbourne Lodge at Windsor. Whilst the country celebrated the victory at Waterloo in 1815, she lived in misery, deprived even of pocket money, constantly spied on and all her letters opened and read.

The year following Waterloo, a new suitor arrived in Prince Leopold of Saxe-Coburg. Whether she was seeking any way out of her predicament, we shall never know but officially it was said that she was 'warm hearted and full of enthusiasm' for him. His proposal accepted, she married him and went to live at Claremont while Marlborough House was being prepared as a town house.

She was, however, to have no long life of happiness. This sad story has a sadder ending. She died giving birth to a stillborn son. Princess Charlotte might have been Queen of England, but her death opened the way for Queen Victoria to come to the throne. Instead of a Victorian era, we might have been remembering the reign of Charlotte, the one time prisoner of Critchel.

26

The Sinking of the *Hood*

ON 4th November 1914 my grandfather, a naval pensioner recalled to serve on the Boom Defence of Portland Harbour, announced as he left home – 'I'm going to sink the *Hood*', and it turned out to be a day to be remembered. My Cornish-born grandfather had served as a Chief Petty Officer when the Navy was powered by sail and steam, and his dry humour was in complete contrast to his half-Spanish wife's sharp tongue. He would tell you in deep sincerity how the King at Portland had once asked him the way to the ablutions and, coming to attention, he had replied 'How many funnels has she Sir?'

The breakwaters forming Portland Harbour had three entrances, one a south facing gap, and readers with nautical knowledge will be asking why a harbour wall was so designed when it was an invitation to the enemy to stand off and fire a torpedo straight into the naval base. The simple truth is that Portland was planned as a harbour of refuge at the beginning of the 19th century and the torpedo had not yet then been invented. That weapon of destruction made its debut in 1867. Portland was mid-way between Portsmouth and Plymouth and conveniently almost north of the French naval base of Cherbourg, 60 miles away. The planned unnatural harbour, a long wall formed by blocks of Portland stone, not only provided a calm refuge for a whole fleet but also offered some protection to Weymouth. By the time the Great War started in 1914 that southern entrance, which had been a short cut to the open sea, was vulnerable to torpedo attacks by German U-boats.

The Admiralty decided to tow the old 14,000 ton battleship *Hood* into the entrance and sink her by opening the sea-cocks, to block the gap. At the end of hostilities, the idea was to pump her out and raise her. The *Hood*, built in 1891, had been removed from the fighting list two years before the First World War had started and had been used as a torpedo target.

There has been much controversy as to whether she was sunk with her guns and boats still aboard, but a photograph in David Burnett's excellent book, *A Dorset Camera 1914 to 1945*, dispels all doubts. The *Hood* was shorn of all guns and boats but the turrets were left intact. She also carried her masts and unusual smoke stacks mounted side by side.

The sea-cocks were opened at slack water but the *Hood* sank too slowly and, getting out of control, the order was given to blow a hole in her side. The unstable hull, shorn of armour-plating, immediately turned turtle and sank upside-down. And there she is to this day, an excellent breeding ground for whiting and bass, the reddened rusting hull looking like a slumbering whale.

So the old *Hood* ended her 23 years service proudly, even if in an undignified manner, helping to defend the Portland naval base from a new and ruthless weapon of war – the torpedo.

My grandfather ended that day listening to the scorn of my grandmother who made a point of telling the whole street about the operation, adding, 'Anything that old fool had a finger in was sure to be bungled' – at least I think that is the word she used!

27

Dorset's Dick Whittington

OF all the pantomime fairy stories, Dick Whittington is many people's favourite. Dick Whittington and his enormous cat sitting by the milestone listening to Bow Bells bidding him to return to London and fortune, is a precious memory of many a childhood and, of course, it was based on fact.

Dorset has a story very similar to that of Dick's. The story begins in the pleasant little Victorian seaside resort of Swanage. A poor boy working deep in the quarries of the Purbecks, with only a few coppers in his pocket, asked the captain of a ship transporting stone and marble to London if he might have a passage to the Metropolis. He was a strong and likeable lad and the captain, taking pity, accepted him aboard ... refusing the coppers the boy offered. In London he found fame and fortune and was eventually responsible for rebuilding much of London in the early 19th century. His name was John Mowlem. The great construction firm he founded is one of those who set up their signs in three feet letters, and few have not at some time contemplated the name 'MOWLEM'.

George III was King when John Mowlem was born in 1789. Swanage was but a village engaged in fishing, and the waterfront was dominated by the great banks of stone and marble brought to the shore for transporting to London. Both found their way into the structures of Cathedrals and Abbeys up and down the land.

As a boy he worked with other members of his family in the famous Tilly Whim quarry. He helped lower the stone blocks down the steep cliff face into the waiting barges, and gazed out from the cave mouth and dreamed of crossing those waters. He was 18 when he gave in to his restlessness and made his deal with the sea captain.

We can only imagine his excitement when he watched the rocks of Old Harry and the chalk cliffs drop astern as the vessel headed east, around the Isle of Wight, up Channel and into the Thames estuary. What were his thoughts as he saw the skyline of London for the first time – knowing he had but ninepence in his pocket?

He was not long without a job and, joining a firm of masons and builders, was soon promoted to foreman. Mowlem never looked back and eventually, with a small amount of capital, started his own business. It was as a road builder that he made his fortune. London was tired of cobbled and muddy streets and Mowlem did much to renew them. He did not find the streets paved with gold, but repaved them in marble.

Without an heir, he took his young nephew, George Burt, into the business – making him a partner. A third partner, a Yorkshire man 'of the best type', married George Burt's sister to complete a very family business.

In 1844, when he was 55 years old, John Mowlem retired from the business and came home to his native Swanage, where he devoted the rest of his life to good works and the rebuilding of his town, which he personally supervised. The poor boy who left with 9 heavy Georgian pennies in his pocket returned to take up a grand house, and had his own stables and coach-house. As a Justice of the Peace, he drove to Wareham on session days in a smart brougham drawn by a fine pair of horses.

Amongst his benefactions was the mill pond, on the side of the hill near the church, and the Mowlem Institute built as a reading room 'for the benefit and mutual improvement of the working classes'. Of local stone, it survived for a century until being replaced by the Mowlem Theatre in 1966.

John Mowlem in Swanage and George Burt, now running

the business in London, continued their benefactions. Together they promoted a Bill in Parliament, at their own expense, to get a railway from Swanage to Wareham, but Mowlem was long dead before George Burt successfully saw its fruition.

It is, however, the incredible museum of bits and pieces of old London, which decorate the streets of Swanage, that is their memorial. These fragments were brought to the Dorset resort as ballast in the ships returning to fetch more stone for the Metropolis.

On the southern shore at Peveril stands a strange faceless clock tower. It was originally built in the 'Perpendicular or best period of Gothic architecture' as a memorial to the Duke of Wellington, and stood in the southern approach to London Bridge. The lower part was a telegraph station, and the illuminated clock with four dials was made for the Great Exhibition of 1851. It was a bad time-keeper, owing to the rumbling traffic passing by, and was a poor tribute to the Duke who was a martinet for punctuality. Soon the tower was obstructing traffic and the police pronounced it 'an unwarrantable obstruction'. Mowlem's offer to remove it was accepted and, in 1866, it was dismantled and each stone numbered and brought by boat to Swanage. The errant clock never arrived.

The Town Hall boasts the original ornate 17th century frontage of the Mercers Hall in Cheapside. Elaborately carved, it had been erected soon after the Great Fire of London and, when the Hall was rebuilt, it was found to be cheaper to copy the stonework than clean the old, grimed by London smog. Burt dismantled it and built it into the new Swanage Town Hall, and in the sea air the stonework has cleaned itself. The London building was completely destroyed by enemy action in 1941.

Ornate London lamp-posts bearing the names of London boroughs lined the seafront until they were replaced some years ago, and some bollards dotted around the town were the barrels of unwanted cannons.

John Mowlem's great joke was a granite column erected on

the seafront to commemorate the destruction of the Danish fleet by King Alfred in AD 877. It was surmounted by 4 cannonballs, though gunpowder was not invented until 500 years after the battle!

Mowlem erected the little prison cell behind the Town Hall, and friends of prisoners locked up for the night often fed beer to them, with the aid of a clay pipe inserted in the key hole.

The most remembered offering to the Dorset resort is the stone globe of the world presented by George Burt and erected on the cliffside at Durlston Head. Constructed in 1887 at Greenwich, it is ten feet in diameter, weighs 40 tons and consists of 15 segments of Portland stone. It was brought to Swanage by sea.

It would seem that John Mowlem and his nephew George Burt were determined that Swanage would never forget them, and a pleasant day's outing will take you around the town seeking out Mowlem and Burt fragments, including strange rhymes carved into stonework.

John Mowlem never returned to London to become Lord Mayor, nor for that matter, did he become the humble Mayor of seaside Swanage ... but his name will be long revered in this pleasant little Dorset town.

28

The End of the World is Nigh!

TO be told at the tender age of 11 years that the end of the world is imminent and that it will begin in your home town next week is a fearsome thought. When, in May 1928, a former Baptist Minister prophesied the Great Armageddon, it was a field day for the popular Sunday press. The Rev. J. W. Potter, who had charge of St. Luke's Chapel, South Norwood, which he said was the Catholic cathedral of Christian spiritualism, confirmed that he had received a number of spirit messages regarding a period of world tribulation. One message implied that Weymouth would be destroyed by a giant tidal wave at 3.53 p.m. on Tuesday 29th May, and it would be the harbinger of an eight-year period of world tribulation.

It was the Whitsun Holiday weekend and, after the spate of national newspaper coverage, the town authorities were worried that it would affect the influx of visitors although only one – a man of over 80 – was reported to have left town.

However, the authorities prevailed upon the Press Association to issue a statement to the effect that 'whether or not Weymouth is to be destroyed by a tidal wave on Tuesday, as has been predicted, the town is very much alive today and is thronged with visitors'.

High spot of the coverage was a mention in the leader column of the prestigious London *Times*, couched in that paper's famous style under the heading 'Pyramidal'. 'The end of the world, or even of that far from contemptible portion of it which is situate in Southern England and includes the pleasant town of Weymouth, is an event that must not pass unregarded. ... The man who takes no chances is probably to be found today not only considering alternative routes North but speculating upon the originality of modern advertising and wondering whether Weymouth is not as near to the opening of its summer season as Vichy is to Glozel. ... While to inconveniences expected to accompany it compel attention, courtesy insists respected anticipation no less. Few cataclysms have the civility to announce themselves. The best they are generally capable of is to discover prophets after the event. This time disaster approaches with elaborate urbanity.'

So much for the intellectual approach but what about me? I was then eleven years old, frightened, puzzled and perplexed. I read the news as it unfolded each day. Vicars preached sermons on the Whit Sunday. The Rev. F. W. Coryton, Vicar of St. John's on the seafront, told his parishioners to trust in the Lord and quoted Psalm 112, Verse 7, 'He shall not be afraid of evil tidings, his heart is fixed trusting in the Lord'. And added 'kindly pass this divine assurance to any troubled and anxious soul'.

That did not console me when I read that a man at Wyke had built a canoe which he lodged between his chimney pots all ready for a take-off on the flood. Or when the Mayor, Alderman Bartle Pye, an autocratic-looking gentleman, said he was entertaining a party of Dutchmen on the great day. 'They are used to floods', he quipped. 'Anyway I am lunching aboard their liner *Rhyden* in Portland Harbour so I shall be aboard my own ark'.

The great day dawned following a scarlet sunset the night before, which many thought was an omen. It was a still sunny morning which left Weymouth's famous blue water bay unruffled.

My mother had made no concession to this traumatic day. 'Eat up the white of your egg', she had commanded and, 'Have you washed behind your ears?' 'Does it matter?' I said, and promptly burst into tears.

Those final hours are etched on my mind. Wandering through the streets to the seafront, I saw a notice outside a newsagent's shop – 'Closed for the Cataclysm – Reopen at 6.30 p.m.', it said.

The town fishermen had brought a thresher shark out of cold storage to help collect for their broken nets and, on the hilltop all around the Bay, carloads of holidaymakers were picnicking in places of safety with a grandstand view.

Aimlessly I wandered along the promenade. A large notice proclaimed that the vocalist booked to sing Handel's 'The Trumpets Shall Sound' had declined because he remembered a previous engagement in North Dorset.

At 3.30 p.m. a pilot called Cooper, who gave 2s 6d flips in a Tiger Moth, turned to his mechanic and said 'Come on, Carpenter, let's go up and chuck a few loops and entertain the crowds.' Ten minutes later he had spiralled into the sea and was killed. With the throng, I raced to the spot where the plane had crashed. The crumpled wreckage lay in a heap on the water like a giant bird shot out of the sky, and small craft converged on the tragic scene. Shocked, I turned away and, looking at the face of the Jubilee clock on the promenade, I saw it was registering 4.20 p.m. The cataclysm had become an anti-climax as the aircraft crashed and life was still going on. I raced home relieved and happy.

29

The Sheriff who Erred

ONE of the most amusing legends in Dorset's long history concerned the colourful 16th century squire, Sir Thomas More, who in a moment of aberration, and high alcohol intake, set free all the prisoners from Dorchester Jail.

A story to warm the hearts of most Englishmen and women who will at some time have felt the urge to commit an outrageous act when fortified with a few drinks.

An heiress of the Melplash family brought the West Dorset Mansion at Melplash to Walter More of Marnhull and it was a descendant of Walter's, Sir Thomas More, who eventually inherited this fine mansion, described by a Dorset historian as a 'house worthy of the princely days of the squires'.

Sir Thomas must not be confused with his more famous namesake and contemporary and was a jovial man who enjoyed a joke or prank as well as his share of alcoholic drink. Henry VIII was on the throne at the time and our Sir Thomas was created Sheriff of Dorset.

After a heavy drinking spree he must have taken leave of his senses or maybe it was the result of a wager with his drinking friends, but he decided that it would be a jolly prank to open the doors of the County Jail and set all the prisoners free.

It must be imagined that he galloped off yelling with delight surprising the villagers of Toller Porcorum and Maiden Newton and after the 15 mile journey arrived at Dorchester with none of his enthusiasm for the prank diminished. Dorchester in the 16th century did not look quite as it does today but his final gallop would have taken him downhill through the town to the jail which, at that time, was at the eastern end.

His enthusiasm rubbed off on the residents who, sensing that something was about to happen, followed the horseman down town. Jovial Sir Thomas, his face aglow with excitement and ale, requested that the astonished warders should open the gates. Sensing their reluctance to carry out the command, he ordered the sullen and sober warders to carry out his order. In Tudor days a Sheriff's command had to be obeyed and they turned the keys and one by one the prisoners moved towards the entrance – at first with natural uncertainty. The Dorchester crowds gathered behind the Sheriff, cheering with him and encouraging the prisoners to get moving. Soon the surprised internees realised that the invitation to freedom was real, and highwaymen, sheep-stealers and pickpockets raced for open country and concealment before someone had a change of mind.

Sheriff More went home to sleep but the warders sat around in their empty prison, wondering how long the news would take to reach London. Naturally the authorities at the Capital took a very serious view of the Dorset exploit and a subdued and sobered Sir Thomas realised that he would have to seek a Pardon from the King. He sought the aid of the Lord Treasurer, Lord Paulet, who helped him to obtain this Pardon but, as can be imagined, Lord Paulet wanted his 'pound of flesh'. Neither did he rate his service cheaply and Sir Thomas not only had to give his daughter's heavily dowered hand in marriage to Lord Paulet's second son, but also Melplash Manor, which was part of her inheritance.

It is not known whether Sir Thomas More regretted his wild spree, but a memorial to the fact that it really happened was perpetuated over the chimney piece in the hall of Melplash Manor where the Arms of the Paulet family and their motto 'Aimez loyaulte' dated 1604 can, I believe, still be seen in the refurbished mansion.

30

The Naughty Knight of Shaftesbury

IT is comforting to know that nuns who choose to follow their Lord earn respect from almost every section of the community. The out-and-out lout will step off the pavement and moderate his language in their presence. Men often avoid their eyes lest the look is misunderstood and it is difficult to be completely at ease when engaging these ladies in conversation.

It was Bing Crosby, a film star renowned for his love songs and a screen image of gentleness and goodness, who nearly let the side down. As a Roman Catholic Father in *The Bells of St. Mary's* he was shown falling in love with a beautiful nun. However, the hour was saved and they parted realising they could have no future together, saddening millions of emotional cinema-goers all over the world. His lapse could be forgiven as the nun was portrayed by the beautiful Ingrid Bergman.

The naughty knight, Sir Osbert Gifford, had no such excuse in the 13th century scandal at Shaftesbury when he engaged a couple of naughty nuns in what he hoped could be a naughty night! The Abbey on the hilltop of North Dorset was founded in AD 888 by King Alfred who gave the church of Shaftesbury 100 hides of land 'to the Honour of God and the Holy Virgin and for the health of his own soul'. His daughter, Ethelgede, was the first Abbess and the Abbey flourished until the 16th century.

Over the years many of Shaftesbury's nuns came from influential and wealthy families, bringing their wealth to swell the Abbey's coffers.

We do not know if the two naughty nuns were wealthy or just

high-spirited young girls enjoying a spree, but obviously the randy Sir Osbert Gifford saw his chance and his lust overruled his sense of responsibility and respect.

He stole the two nuns from the Nunnery. The Archbishop of Canterbury, on a visit to Shaftesbury in 1285, excommunicated Sir Osbert Gifford for stealing them, absolving him on these conditions: 'that he should never after come into a nunnery or into the company of nuns; that he should for three Sundays together, be stripped and whipped in his parish church of Wilton and as many times in the market and parish church of Shaftesbury, and fast a certain number of months, and not wear a shirt for three years, and not take upon him the habit or title of a knight, nor wear any apparel but a russet colour, with lamb or sheep skins, and he should restore the nuns to their convent to undergo like punishment. All which he bound himself by oath to do.'

Many male readers may ask themselves was it really worth it, but historian Sir Frederick Treves, a kinder man, was more concerned with the harsh punishment given the nuns, although he admits it was obvious they were not stolen by force but very willing accessories 'and there was probably much unseemly giggling before and after the act'. Sir Frederick particularly disliked the rough coarse apparel they were instructed to wear in their disgrace. He recorded: 'It is a base thing that a loutish sheep hide should brush a cheek which knew only the tender touch of a wimple of white linen'.

Through several centuries the Abbey on these North Dorset heights became famous and the town of Shaftesbury with it.

The Abbey's greatness which began with a procession ended with one, when in 1539 Elizabeth Zouch, the last Abbess, led her 55 sobbing nuns from the Abbey to descend the hill for the last time in the disastrous year of the Reformation when Henry VIII dissolved the great religious Houses of England. She had been at Shaftesbury for over 40 years – in fact many nuns spent their whole lives in the Abbey.

Henry VIII sold the great abbey to the Arundell family who demolished it and built houses with the stone.

31

Dorset's Pitchfork Army

AS the Civil War raged up and down the country between 1642 and 1646, the affrays between Royalists and Parliamentarians provided pages of history for the county historians. Although no major battle was fought in Dorset, this gentle Shire county was of strategic importance to both sides – being situated between London and the very Loyalist West of England. Lulworth Castle was garrisoned for the King but Cromwell's men seized it and stole the lead off the roof. Lady Bankes, with her staff, fought off attacks on Corfe Castle, in the absence of her husband, but it eventually fell to treachery and the Roundheads blew it up. Castles at Sherborne and Portland were also besieged and taken.

As the opposing armies roamed back and forth across the countryside, the village folk were the prime sufferers although most of them could not care less who was winning or even knew what it was all about. However, they did know that their villages were being constantly raped and crops ruined. No sooner had the fields been sown than an army would march over it and set up a camp. If the crops had reached the harvesting stage, a passing regiment would tear it up to boost their stocks and leave the fruit trees bare. The farmers dare not go to the fields with their horses lest, as they toiled, passing soldiery would steal the horses from the shafts of the carts. Fighting men not only milked the cows, but often led them off marching in their ranks until a chance came to slaughter them for food. The simple country folk also had to keep an eye on their women.

Feeling alone and helpless the wealthy landowners, farmers, farmhands and even the clergy decided if you cannot beat them join them, and formed yet a third army called the Clubmen. It was a Dad's Army Home Guard style organisation, determined to fight whichever side wrecked their estates.

Many clergy came forward as leaders of this strange army, probably seeking a little excitement from their strict lives.

Several Shire Counties formed Clubmen Armies but the organisation was strongest in Dorset – no doubt egged on by the Welds, Ashley-Coopers and Digbys, all large estate owners whose lands had suffered by the pillage imposed by the opposing Civil War armies.

In May 1645 a large meeting of interested parties was held on Cranborne Chase. Those of us who have lived through a time when, during the Second World War, the Home Guard was told to equip itself with pikes and carry out drills with broom handles, are not in any position to laugh at the motley crowd of farm folk and tradesmen who assembled that May morning on the Chase armed with clubs, swords, billhooks, pitchforks and any other sharp implements that could be manually wielded. Nearly 350 years later, we must be allowed a smile because it is not recorded whether the groups were formed according to their weapons, so that the men could go home and boast that they were in the Pitchfork Platoon or the Billhook Brigade.

Four thousand men attended this meeting and another was held at Badbury Rings. A peace-keeping association was formed 'to assist one another in the mutual defence of our liberties and properties against all plunderers and all other unlawful violence'. The name Clubmen was not adopted because of their weapons, but symbolised the fact that they had clubbed together to protect their land. They adopted this slogan and emblazoned it on their banners:

'If you offer to plunder and take our cattle
Be assured we will give you battle.'

The Parliamentarians were the main adversaries of the Dorset men, but during the early summer of 1645 groups of them had minor clashes with both sides. In July an attack on the Roundhead H.Q. at Sturminster Newton resulted in deaths on both sides.

The minor skirmishes continued. Many of the actions were led by the Rev. Thomas Bravell, Rector of Compton Abbas, supported by the Rectors of Pulham, Chettle and St. Peter's Shaftesbury. In August the Clubmen became a nuisance to Sir Thomas Fairfax whose Roundhead army was beginning the seige of Sherborne Castle. Sir Thomas decided enough was enough and delegated Oliver Cromwell, his Lieutenant General, to deal with this 'nuisance'.

Cromwell, an accomplished diplomat, 'smooth-talked' the Clubmen whom he captured on Duncliffe Hill near Shaftesbury and promised their leaders that they would not be ill treated or plundered again. They went home contented but 2,000 Clubmen on the ramparts of Hambledon Hill above Shroton, south of Shaftesbury, were made of sterner stuff. From their lofty position atop the steep sloped hill, they were difficult to approach and, although Cromwell tried to reason with them, they were adamant – probably because the tough Rev. Bravell had threatened to shoot anyone who surrendered.

They had litle chance against the drilled military force who eventually attacked them from the rear, and the frightened Clubmen came running, rolling and falling down the steep hillside – many of them sliding unceremoniously on their backsides. Twenty were killed and 300 were rounded up and locked in the church for the night. Next morning Cromwell talked to them and pointed out the error of their ways. It must have been degrading for poor Thomas Bravell being preached at in church! The 300 decided that Oliver Cromwell was not such a bad chap after all and, promising to be good in future, they returned to their villages.

Cromwell reported to Sir Thomas Fairfax at Sherborne that the rebellion had been quelled and pleaded on the Clubmen's behalf, not only admiring their spirit but probably having some sympathy with their cause. 'They are poor silly creatures', he reported, 'and they promise to be very dutiful for the time to come and will be hanged before they come out again.' Even the Rev. Bravell was forgiven and that seemed to be the end of the Clubmen. But I expect many of them retold the story of their summer of discontent to grandchildren years later, and I often sit in the little church at Iwerne Courtney and wonder what the 300 talked about on that August evening three and a half centuries ago.

32

Father Christmas without a Hood

THE presentation of Father Christmas takes many forms in English stores during the annual festival, but the arrival of the benevolent gentleman with the jolly red face at Bournemouth each year had a charisma that was unique for over half a century. Perhaps it was due to the fact that Beales of Bournemouth always claimed to be the first store to commercialise Father Christmas, and presented him in spectaculars of taste and beauty – sparing no expense. After the last War, the parade annually encouraged thousands of people to line the streets of Bournemouth, coming in from towns and villages over a very large area; a return to sanity after years of war.

Bournemouth's Father Christmas never wore a hood but sported flowing white locks. That situation arose because Mrs. John Beale, who made the first robe in 1885, could find no way of fixing a hood onto her handmade costume of velvet trimmed on skirt and cuffs with white bands of imitation ermine. Consequently, Beales had to purchase an expensive beard and wig.

Even if their Father Christmas was not the first to officially proceed to a store, he most certainly was the first to arrive by aeroplane at a time when very few people had taken to the air.

In 1912 he took off in an open cockpit plane from a field at the bottom of Pokesdown Hill, flew very low over the store in central Bournemouth and waved to the crowds beneath him. Flying was considered very dangerous so a member of the family, Cyril Beale, donned the robes on that occasion. Between the Wars the event grew in importance, each year having a new theme with the floats prepared by the store's own display people, and on the great November day the store's staff donned costumes to take part in the procession, nearly a mile long and sometimes interspersed with three brass bands.

Early in the 1950s I donned the red robe to create an inside story on Father Christmas. The gear was so elaborate, from the golden boots to the face-fitting wig and beard, that I began to believe I was Father Christmas and was still fulfilling the role 15 years later when Selective Employment Tax caused the axing of the Beales' event.

I was often accused of being 'very happy' during those rides and I must admit that, with the whole station staff arriving bearing pints of ale to take wine with Father Christmas during the make-up session, I was in a happy, festive mood when the coach arrived. In reality, it was often an emotional and traumatic experience. There were people on that route who were in the same position over the whole 15 years, some parents still present long after the children had lost interest. Each year there were letters asking for personal waves, and the very special case of an ailing child who eventually passed away. The parents came alone that year and, as we waved, it was special for us both.

The cheering crowds could not hear the quarrelling and bad language going on atop the coach as the horn-blower quarrelled with a bad-tempered coachman who brought his elegant horses from London. He was more used to appearing in costume films and felt that the Bournemouth parade was a little beneath his dignity.

In later years a team of greys from Tom Sampson's farm at Ringwood was used. The red-cheeked jovial driver was proud of his colourful cloak and cocked hat and revelled in the occasion. Turning with a broad facial beam on one journey he quipped: 'Christmas, I'd look a right Charlie behind a plough in this lot.' Charlie Newham was a warm-hearted bucolic character and a rare wit. I was benevolently waving to a large crowd of young people outside the Winter Gardens – 'Put yer 'and down Christmas,' he shouted above the cheering, 'they ain't come to see you – they wants them Beatles!' Those were the happy years. The coach always paused at the foot of Bath Hill so that the walking procession could reach the crest of Exeter Road. The wobbling bottoms of the proud Percherons – Gilbert, Flower, Molly and Suzy – stilled for a few moments. The horsey aroma from the sweating bodies was wafted by the crisp seaside breeze, until Charlie – with a 'Way up' – trotted the heavy coach up the hill.

Once the run was mistimed and the coach drove through the ranks of a brass band who could not hear it coming because of their music. Bandsmen and instruments scattered in all directions – never had the *Happy Wanderer* ended in such discord!

33

The King who Loved Sea Bathing

ONE of the exciting pleasures of the 20th century is sea bathing, and most people in their younger years have enjoyed beach parties and the excitement of togetherness in the near nude on the hot days of summer . . . or just relaxing to get the all-over handsome tan. This refreshing recreation had its beginnings in the Dorset seaside resort of Weymouth when, in 1789, the eccentric King George III entered the sea as a cure. Affairs of State had been worrying him and the King had suffered a breakdown.

He was following the advice of the Bath philanthropist, Ralph Allen. In 1763 Ralph had become very sick and his physician advised 'a treatment so extreme and so strange that it savoured of madness'. It consisted of bathing the bare body in the open sea. Allen chose Weymouth for his daring experiment, and had a six-sided box built on a platform supported by large wooden wheels which a horse could tow into the sea, and from which he could step into the water. The cure worked and the builder of the hut became a rich man because two decades later sea bathing had become so popular that the beach was swarming with these machines resembling an army of Georgian Daleks.

The Royal bather in 1789 put a final seal of approval on sea immersion, but the ceremony was not to be taken lightly. The royal physician, Dr. Grisborne, advised that the King 'should prepare for the ordeal by special observances'. He had to take warm salt baths in his room until he was sufficiently hardened to 'dip boldly into the open Channel'.

There was a touch of Gilbert and Sullivan comic opera in the scenario of the Royal bathe. We are dependent on the cartoonists of the day who showed the King with ladies holding towels around him as he stepped into the water. Townsfolk lined the shore cheering and waving flags and, as the King submerged beneath a wave, a band concealed in a neighbouring bathing machine struck up the National Anthem, *God Save Great George Our King*. It must have been a tight squeeze for the musicians, because a couple of corpulent cornet players and a big drum would have left little room for the extending slide of a trombone player, not to mention the horns and the giant brass instruments.

The presence of the Royal household holidaymaking in the area had sent the town mad with joy and excitement. 'God Save the King' was emblazoned on banners across the streets, as well as on the hat bands of children and on sashes around women's waists. Even the bargemen had it written on their cockades.

When the present Prince and Princess of Wales are sometimes portrayed showing irritation when the Press intrude on their private ski-ing holidays, it proves that nothing is new because the Weymouth crowds, overjoyed with having Royalty living in their midst, not only raised their hats and shouted 'God Save the King' every time they passed the Royal party in the streets, but also pressed their noses against the windows of the Royal residence, the Gloucester Lodge, to get a glimpse of the King at home.

It was the informality of the Royals in holiday mood which pleased the Weymouth people. It was shown in the town Mayor's address of welcome: 'The sight of their Monarch is always grateful to a loyal people, but is never more so than, when laying aside the awful splendour of a throne, he condescends to appear amongst them clothed in the more pleasing, because better known, character of domestic life.' However, Mayor Arbuthnot was soon in trouble when he failed to kneel before the King and Queen. Severely reprimanded, he protested: 'But I cannot kneel, I have a wooden leg.' A story which the King probably recalled with gusto at many a private dinner party.

The Royal family did all the things that ordinary folk do at the seaside. They gathered shells, the King enjoyed boating trips and the three Princesses bathed frequently and 'were much delighted with their ablutions'. The King visited the Welds at Lulworth Castle and made a special journey to Windspit to see the spot where the East Indiaman *Halsewell* was wrecked with great loss of life a few years previously. Special talent was introduced into the Weymouth theatre.

The King obviously benefited from the Dorset air and not only went back to Windsor refreshed, but returned frequently between 1791 and 1805 to the Gloucester Lodge which was specially built for a Royal summer residence.

Weymouth has never fully recovered from the joy of providing the holiday venue for the Royal Family. They erected a rather pompous statue where the town shopping streets converge onto the seafront. A statue made hideous in recent years when the authorities decided to paint it in gaudy colours. The Georgian terraces still line the blue watered bay, of which the King commented on first seeing it: 'I never enjoyed a sight so pleasing', and hotels bear royal names including the Royal Lodge which is now the Gloucester Hotel. Then there is the most famous and unique memory ... the enormous carving in the chalk hill which overlooks the town, depicting the King on a white charger.

Keeping the Royal holiday story alive in the 1980s, the Weymouth authorities presented the famous bathing machine in their Museum. But is it genuine? It appears that the first machine used by the King had the Coat of Arms painted over the door, but a second and rather larger machine was built for the second visit.

Successive owners of the bathing machine fleet charged more for those marked with the Royal insignia, so by the time a Mr. Scrivens took them over at the turn of the century, it would probably have been expedient to label most of them with the crest.

Then came the day when the machines went out of fashion and, too worn to make the bumpy journey into the surf, the Dalek army was sold off. Shorn of their enormous wooden wheels, they found strange last resting places. Many were dotted around the town's allotments serving as tool sheds, and others had a more elegant retirement as garden summer-houses. One of these bearing its Coat of Arms stood overlooking Newtons Cove at Bincleaves. Cliff Chalker, a Weymouth businessman, believes his machine is the genuine Royal box and when the town opened its Museum, he presented it to the authorities. Refurbished and wheels reinstated, it looks as good as new.

34

The Chinese Giant

SOMEWHERE in a corner of a Bournemouth cemetery, in a grave untended and flattened by the course of time, lies the most colourful and certainly the largest character ever to grace the Bournemouth scene.

Chinaman Chang Woo Gow was 8 feet tall and weighed 26 stones. Yet the man who was once the toast of the town and welcomed at social functions, has left nothing to remember him by except a few photographs taken by a Victorian photographer, Robert Day Jnr., in whose arms he died in 1893. Incidentally, it was Robert Day Snr. who gave us a comprehensive history of Victorian Bournemouth in the form of a library of magnificent photographs.

Chang came to London in 1865 from his home in distant Foochow when he was only 19 years of age. Showmen sought him out for their exhibitions and the famous American, Phineas T. Barnum put him on show in the Egyptian Hall in London's Piccadilly. It was originally built as a museum and had an Oriental style facade – so it was an ideal setting for Chang's purposes.

In those days when few Englishmen ventured beyond their island shores – let alone journey to the other side of the world – visitors from the mysterious Orient held a strange fascination. Chang was advertised as the 'Magic Giant' who had 'created a sensation at the Court of the Emperor of China' and was put on display with a Chinese dwarf, Chung Mow, and other Chinamen of normal size.

In his act Chang sat aloft on a high throne clad in a white satin robe, reminiscent of a Buddha, in the hall of a Chinese mansion. The whole cast of the show were dressed in exotic colourful costumes and, with the dwarf at his feet, Chang presented an awe-inspiring spectacle.

The performance was hailed with the tinkling of a bell and as a pianist played in the background Chang slowly rose to his feet and ascended the throne steps to greet his audience. He smiled at everyone, offered his massive hand to some and, at the sounding of a gong, bowed to his astonished admirers and then returned to his throne. It seems very little in exchange for the expensive one, two and three shilling seats, but he packed the house four performances a day. He travelled the world making occasional trips to his homeland and when he finally returned to London in 1880, such was his memory for faces that he remembered people he had met on his first visit. He should have been a rich man but his generosity knew no bounds.

In middle age his health began to fail and, like many others at that time with chest complaints, chose Bournemouth as his place of retirement in 1890. He arrived there and bought a spacious house in Southcote Road called 'Moyuen' where he lived out his life in the residence with specially built doorways and unique furniture including a table 5 ft. tall. His Australian-born wife and two sons were of normal height. He opened his home as a Chinese tea-rooms and sold curios from his Chinese bazaar. Bournemouth, which has always had a soft spot for unusual characters, welcomed Chang. At Mayoral receptions his arrival in full Chinese regalia drew sighs of appreciation as he mingled with the elegantly garbed ladies and aldermen in their colourful red robes.

In 1893 his wife was taken ill and died within a few weeks. The Chinaman lost all will to live and could not speak of her without his eyes filling with tears. Four months later on 5th November, the night of fire-cracker celebration, he called his friend, Robert Day, to his home, begged him to look after his children and, holding his hand, the gentle giant died of a broken heart.

So vast was the crowd that attended his funeral that the Chapel could not hold them all. Many had come to see the largest coffin ever made – 8 feet 4 inches by 2 feet 6 inches. It took 8 pall-bearers to carry him. They laid him to rest beside his wife.

Today his former home is an hotel and his lovely garden a car park. With no relatives left to tend the grave, even the mound under which he was buried has long been flattened and no trace of it remains.

35

The Rhododendrons of Minterne Magna

TO most nature lovers the rhododendron is a large and lovely flower seen in several hues of purple, growing profusely in great banks in woodlands and coastal chines, but few know that it is an international bloom showing itself in hundreds of shapes and styles and colours, and that it can be seen at many seasons of the year. A stud book is kept in which the most important shrubs are registered, and there are almost 1,000 species mostly evergreen and they prefer acid soil.

In a peaceful village at the heart of Dorset, many hundreds of rhododendron types are bred and members of a famous titled family, the Digbys of Dorset, have devoted several lifetimes to preparing one of the most unusual and beautiful gardens in the country, propagating the floral species. The history and success of Minterne Magna will interest even those of us who let our potted geraniums die for lack of water and attention, and wince at the thought of cutting grass on a lawn little larger than a pocket handkerchief.

The first Digby bought Minterne House in 1768 when Captain the Hon. Robert Digby, younger brother of Edward Sixth Baron Digby of nearby Sherborne Castle, moved in. He had a distinguished naval career, was gazetted Rear Admiral in 1779 and later appointed Naval Instructor to George III's son, William. His first impression of Minterne: 'Estate compact but naked and trees not thriving'. He was, however, soon at work creating his garden. He planted two clumps of beeches and got rid of the gardener. He then created a lake, built a bridge, and surrounded the house with plantations.

The planting of those beeches ensured the long-term future of Minterne because one of the things that strikes visitors coming there for the first time is the fact that these magnificent rhododendrons, contrary to most ideas, grow and flower so well under cover of the enormous beech trees that abound in the garden. The explanation appears to be that although the beech is a robber of both soil and light, he does no harm at Minterne owing to the overhead cover being high, while the volume of humus generated by the leaf fall seems to offset the goodness taken out of the ground by the tree. The high average annual rainfall at Minterne of 40 inches, which together with the wind shelter is the greatest asset to a successful rhododendron garden.

The house eventually came to Edward Henry Trafalgar, the 10th Baron Digby, who led the life of an English gentleman taking part in field sports, and public service. The house was found to have dry rot, so Minterne was rebuilt at the turn of the century and when guests came to a garden party in 1908, Admiral Robert's late 18th century garden was mature, and the rhododendron garden laid out in the 1890s was ready to receive new varieties of the blooms.

The present century came in with the Victorian gardening craze of formal bedding still at its height. Minterne, however, by then was luckily well in advance of the times with its firmly established shrub garden, which made an ideal setting for the wonderful discoveries of the many new types of rhododendrons – many from the Himalayas – which were to pour in from the numerous Chinese explorations. Minterne benefited greatly from the work of such collectors as Wilson, Farrer, Forrest, Rock, Kingdon-Ward and the Chinese collector, Professor Hu. They have all produced rhododendrons that have grown into noteworthy plants at Minterne. Expertly tended, the garden now complements the Edwardian house.

In the 1950s Col. the Lord Digby, like the present Lord

Digby – a Lord Lieutenant of Dorset, could boast magnificent cedars two hundred years after the planting . . . one with a girth of 25 ft. He inherited the garden in his early twenties and devoted his life to their improvement, seeing seeds brought from far away China grow into a potential forest. He used seeds collected on several expeditions. Today there are 350 specimens of rhododendron and at least twice as many hybrids.

The visitor who comes to Minterne Magna, a village still as serene and beautiful as it was a century ago, can enjoy such exquisite blooms as The Duchess of Montrose and the Minterne hybrid, Early Star, which blooms in March, and the pink Nobleanum which can be seen in mid-winter . . . and hundreds of other exotic and colourful blooms. Pride of the vast collection is the crimson Lady Digby, produced by mating *R. facetum* from Reginald Farrers' collection with the best form of *strigillosum*.

I visited Minterne Magna on a warm summer afternoon in late June. The present Lord Digby led me through the woods and down the slopes to the banks where the rhododendrons bloomed beside trickling streams and beneath shady trees. Then he left me and I could have happily set up camp and stayed for ever. Forget the traditional stately home garden laid out neat and precise like a grocer's display. Here is a jungle of unbelievable colour with soft green fern underfoot and only the birdsong and stream to destroy the silence.

Two miles down the road is Cerne Abbas with its rude giant cut into the hillside and quaint street market where the tourists converge and linger. But few discover Minterne. You have to seek it out, and here at the family home of the Digbys you can share with them a rare garden and meet the colourful Sheila Moores, Cerisettes, Cynthias, Bodartianums, Blue Tits and Pink Pearls. There is one bloom called plain Arthur Smith, named after the trusted gardener who for 30 years worked side by side with Lord Digby and who, with little help, devoted his life to making Minterne's beautiful garden so special.

36

Adventurer on a Handcart

HOLIDAY voyagers, who came up from Poole to the port of Wareham just after the last war, often contained their laughter as they passed an ancient tall houseboat built in the hull of a traditional Rochester barge moored amongst the reeds. Its owner, a tall erect figure in yachting rig more appropriate to a seagoing gin palace, was elegant and wearing a high rollneck white jersey beneath his reefer jacket, a well-used peaked seaman's cap, and sporting a well trimmed white beard. But the whole seafaring ensemble was made to look slightly ridiculous because on the tip of his nose was a pair of steel pince-nez spectacles.

Few of the giggling trippers realised that this man was Percy Westerman, the famous author of adventure books for boys. The character whose stories introduced decades of pre war youngsters to exotic countries and famous seaports all over the world, and who became a legend in his lifetime, dreaming up his plots on the banks of this peaceful Dorset river. The slow flowing Frome was his Amazon and the reeds on its banks, the jungle. Along the twisting two miles from Wareham Quay to the river's entrance into Poole Harbour, he dreamed up yarns like *His Unfinished Voyage, Held To Ransom, Working Their Passage,* as he indulged in his passion for sailing small boats. Here he invented such characters as Captain Trenarrow and ship's boys Alan Carr and Alaister Duncan – names fondly remembered by schoolboys of the 1920s and 1930s all over the world.

His simple stories, woven around sea scouts and the hardships of boy apprentices on sailing ships, sold over 1½ million copies in this country alone and were translated into eight languages. He drew on his naval background for his knowledge – his father was a Royal Navy Master at Arms – and his style was highly idiosyncratic. One wonders how a typical phrase like 'Simply just wizard, what!' would have appeared when translated into an Eastern European language.

His love of adventure led him to serve in the Marine section of the newly formed RAF near the end of the First World War. Although he had a defective eye, he memorised the reading chart when the doctor left the surgery for a few minutes and so passed the physical! He brought his houseboat to Wareham in the 1920s, and from then until his death in 1959 he produced 3½ books a year.

In the early days the river was a lonely idyllic location for the writer. As he churned out the exciting adventures of his characters, battling with storms and piracy on the high seas, his life style was far more down to earth.

As the Frome became more popular as a boating place, Percy set up moorings for yachtsmen and then formed a yacht club. A 'private and rather exclusive club for Professional Classes only'. With the help of his son, he built two adjoining wooden huts – one for a workshop, and there was a touch of comedy because Percy and his friends objected to a hut which a local gentleman used for bird watching, and wanted him out. They instructed the secretary to write to the gentleman about the state of the hut and warned him that although he was paying rent, he would be responsible for any accident that occurred.

Percy, the author, I am sure, would have had a few of his fictional characters creeping through the reeds at dead of night to burn it down, but Commodore Percy Westerman decided they must go to litigation. In mid-dispute the 'Saga of the Hut' resolved itself . . . it collapsed!

The Redcliffe club house was hardly a palace and such were the primitive toilet facilities, that only male members were entertained. Later, improvements were carried out; the gentlemen's loo consisted of 'half of a large plate glass mirror' (interesting) and the ladies was a 'redundant sea toilet with the bottom beat out'.

An incident which Percy could have turned to advantage was the yacht club's luck in winning a Morecambe Bay Prawner, fitted out as a yacht, in the Irish Hospital Sweepstake. He often planned his plots as he led his river patrol in the club launch up and down the reedy river in the Second World War, when he was a member of the Home Guard.

The author's wife, Florence, 'the girl next door' who he married in 1900, had long been tolerant of her author husband and loved their Spartan life on the river. It was for a half crown bet with her that he could write a better story than those he was reading to their son Jack that decided him to write his first story, *A Boy of Grit*, published in 1908. Well pleased with himself, he embarked on writing stories with enthusiasm and prodigious energy and never looked back.

In the 1950s Florence decided that she and Percy should come ashore, and a comfortable bungalow on Bestwall was purchased. She moved in but Percy stubbornly refused to leave his houseboat. Then fate took a hand and Percy slipped through the rotting timbers, broke his leg and had to take to his bunk to recuperate. Florence took the law into her own hands and, with the aid of her home help, they lifted Percy – wrapped in blankets – on to a builders merchant's handcart and wheeled him through the main street to the bungalow.

The water-borne home which had inspired Percy's writing seemed to grow sad without him and the dilapidated hull was eventually destroyed by controlled explosions in 1961, providing a useful exercise for men of the Junior Leaders Regiment at Bovington, and making a splendid bonfire.

Happily Percy did not know of its end ... an episode that could well have featured in one of his yarns. He passed away in the winter of 1959. Three months later his last book was published – it was called *Mistaken Identity*.

37

The Evil Ring of Knowlton

FEW people pass the ruined church at Knowlton on the Wimborne to Cranborne road without making further investigation. A Christian church at the heart of a pagan shrine is unique.

I discovered it on a Saturday of showers and sunshine 50 years ago. Winter sun on this crisp morning spotlighted the ruin which was backgrounded by a black thundercloud mass speeding away to the north. I reached for a camera to record the phenomenon and, coming closer, discovered that the Norman ruin with a square tower added in the 15th century was beautifully created from Purbeck stone, flint and heath-sand. The whole ruin was cloaked in ivy, the green leaves trying to hide the sadness of this decaying edifice.

Feeling a compelling urge to enter this little church, I spent half-an-hour cutting away cruel brambles which formed an outer protection for the church and, coming into the nave, wished I had stayed outside. It was not the crumbling walls or the pungent aroma of rot and damp that oppressed me, but the intense cold. It was like stepping into a butcher's cold storage room and, gasping for breath, I made a quick exit.

Some months later I recalled the incident to some friends. 'That is a place of evil,' said one, 'The outer ring is steeped in our religious past – it dates back 4,000 years to the Bronze Age and is supposed to have been the scene of human sacrifices, in fact many skeletons have been found there.'

Still in my late teens, I had not given much thought to

strange encounters, things that go bump in the night and communications with spirits ... there were far too many live experiences taking my attention. I had read about Borley Rectory and its sinister ghostly happenings, but believed that all these events had a logical explanation.

Long after the War, I again felt the urge to return to Knowlton and, by this time, had learned something of its awesome history. Knowlton – old English for 'a tun by a knowl' – was once an important village. The oval-shaped ring is a well preserved sacred circle. Its diameter is about 350 ft. and a deep cut ditch inside the bank, 35 ft. wide, is still well marked. The earthwork encloses a flat area of land with two entrances. The bank is 12 ft. high and, for miles around, flat Cranborne Chase countryside, now farmland, is dotted with burial mounds. The later Church of the Christian religion had its services brought to an abrupt end when the congregation was wiped out by the Black Death, and later the Parish was absorbed into Horton. For some strange reason the Church was repaired in the early 18th century but unused, and the slow rot set in.

Then I discovered that I was in good company with my fears. The famous archaeologist, Jacquetta Hawkes, visited Knowlton and she found its atmosphere 'oppressive'. She said, 'There is some peculiar influence in the air of this place, an influence which might be called a taint.'

On my second visit the Department of the Environment had rejuvenated the site – the ivy had been torn off and the church stonework cleaned up. Visitors are free to wander in and out of the old ruin, and the area around has the grass cut into tidy lawns and is designated a picnic spot, but I could not bring myself to enter the building. I have been back three more times and still have not overcome my fear, and the strange thing is that I have never seen anyone picnicking within those ancient earth walls. The environmentalists keep it neat and tidy but to me it is still an awesome place.

There is a strange sequel to this yarn. A few years ago I trespassed into a disused dilapidated Dorset mansion, used as a witches coven. I photographed the room where a large circle was staked out and various garments of underwear lay scattered amongst the dust and the strange symbols chalked on the floor. For only the second time in my life I felt that ice-box grip around my shoulders, causing me to shudder and catch my breath and to beat a hasty retreat!

38

Massacre at Portland

A sad message decorating a weathered tombstone on the heights of Portland is witness to the fact that the activities of the press gangs, who forcibly carried off men to boost the armed forces in the 18th century, were not quite the exciting events portrayed in adventure stories and swashbuckling films.

Pressing men into service was very necessary because there were few volunteers for the intense hardships of living conditions aboard naval vessels.

The Naval press gangs were not fussy how they obtained the men, sometimes bludgeoning drunks in bars and carrying them off, and for each man so captured, the gangs earned handsome bounties.

The stone records that Mary Way 'was shot by some of a Press Gang and died of her wounds the 21st May following, aged 21 years.' Her death was the awful conclusion to what is known as the 'Easton Massacre'.

It all began when the 36-gun frigate *Aigle* anchored in Weymouth Bay on 1st April 1803, an April Fool's Day long to be remembered. Word soon got around that this was a 'hot press' and families set about hiding their menfolk from the terrible consequences of capture. Captain George Wolfe came ashore and conferred with the Mayor and Admiral of the Port of Weymouth and Melcombe Regis, Edward Tucker Steward, obtaining a promise from him that he would give all assistance to the 'press' – a promise that the Captain must have realised would never be honoured.

Dorset had the reputation of being one of the hardest counties in England in which to press gang men and, locally, the male population could scurry to the caves and quarries of Portland and hide for weeks on end with a little prior notice, a fact which the Mayor pointed out. He had to promise that local constables would assist the naval party but on 2nd April, when police help was called for, they were all strangely 'engaged on other duties'.

Captain Wolfe made his landing on Chesil Beach, at the foot of Portland's great mass, in the early hours of 2nd April. With 50 well armed seamen and marines, he found an armed posse on the beach – many of them with weapons washed up when three transports carrying troops to the West Indies were wrecked in a gale a few years before. The conflict on the beach was short and sharp, the untrained locals being no match for the drilled naval party. Only two men were captured – one, James Way, was the brother of the girl who, in a few hours, would be fatally wounded. The rest fled up the steep slope to Tophill. On the order of Captain Wolfe the Press Gang followed and he must have later regretted that instruction because, on the top of the island, the locals were in their element. Their local knowledge enabled them to use the quarries and scurry into hiding like rats retreating down their holes.

With the thought that their bounties would be the less if the marines did not make a quick capture, there was a bloody riot at Easton. Several hundred islanders fought their hearts out and, so determined were they to avoid capture, that later nine men from the crew of the *Aigle* were discharged from the Service as a consequence of terrible injuries inflicted upon them. Whether an order was given is not known, but the marines opened fire on the crowd in an attack which has been described as a massacre. At the end of the affray, four Portlanders were dead: quarrymen Richard Flann and Alexander Andrews, blacksmith William Lano and 21 year old Mary Way.

By this time, Captain Wolfe had problems. Apart from

getting his wounded back down the hill, the press had got out of hand. Also he wanted to be first to give his account of the events to the authorities. He despatched Lt. Francis Hastings (who later became the Earl of Huntingdon) and Midshipman John Fortescue Morgan to London in haste to inform the Admiralty. But on arrival at Weymouth they were promptly arrested by Mayor Stewart and committed to Dorchester Gaol for alleged murder. After an inquest, the Coroner recorded a verdict of 'Wilful Murder' against Captain Wolfe, Lt. Hastings, Midshipman Morgan and ten marines and they were bailed until the Dorchester Summer Assize of 1803.

During the months of waiting, Captain Wolfe gained favour with the Admiralty and as it was a politically bad time to show the British Navy in a bad light, the result of the trial was a foregone conclusion. The four eminent judges not only rejected the evidence of the surgeon attending Mary Way that before she died the girl declared Captain Wolfe was the person who shot her, but also ignored the pleas of the Dorchester attorney who represented the Portland families. The verdict was 'Not Guilty'. Captain Wolfe was, however, reprimanded and told he had made a mistake in making contact with the Mayor of Weymouth when acting under an order from the King in Council. Apart from that, said the Judges, Captain Wolfe had acted in self-defence! Portlanders were angered at the verdict and received much sympathy within the county.

In a moment of remorse, Captain Wolfe had released James Way, captured at Chiswell, because of his sister's critical condition. That left the press gang with three captured men at the cost of the deaths of four islanders, and nine members of their own raiding party so mutilated that they were discharged from the Service.

Bibliography

A Dorset Camera 1855–1914 David Burnett. (Dovecote Press)
Stories from Dorset History Alan J. Miller. (The English Press)
Anymore for the Skylark David Chalk.
Wreck and Rescue on the Dorset Coast Grahame Farr. (D. Bradford Barton Ltd.)
Ebb-tide at Poole John Hillier. (Poole Historical Trust)
Smuggling in Hampshire and Dorset Geoffrey Morley. (Countryside Books)
The Highways & Byways of Dorset Sir Frederick Treves. (Macmillan & Co Ltd.)
Curiosities of Swanage David Lewer & J. Bernard Calkin. (The Gavin Press)
The Bournemouth Song Book Cumberland Clark. (Wilding & Son Ltd.)
Redclyffe Yacht Club, The First Fifty Years. Don Birchan
Rhododendron & Camellia Year Book 1956. The Royal Horticultural Society